N

E

S

Fairypedia

DK Publishing

LONDON, NEW YORK, MUNICH,
MELBOURNE, AND DELHI

Editor SHANNON BEATTY
Designers BILL MILLER AND JESSICA PARK
Managing Art Editor MICHELLE BAXTER
Publishing Director BETH SUTINIS
DTP Coordinator KATHY FARIAS
Production Manager NANCY ROBERTS

Writer ALISHA NIEHAUS
Picture Researcher CHRISSY MCINTYRE
Fairy Consultant EDAIN MCCOY

First Edition, 2009
09 10 11 10 9 8 7 6 5 4 3 2 1
Published in the United States

by DK Publishing
375 Hudson Street,
New York, New York 10014

DK books are available at special discounts for bulk purchases
for sales promotions, premiums, fund-raising, or educational use.
For details, contact:

DK Publishing Special Markets
375 Hudson Street, New York, NY 10014
SpecialSales@dk.com

A complete catalog record for this title is available
from the Library of Congress
ISBN 978-0-7566-5095-7

Color reproduction by Colourscan, Singapore

Printed and bound in China by Hung Hing

Discover more at www.dk.com

ONTENTS

How To Use This Book

Hi, I'm Jenny, and my brother James and I sorta made this book in secret. You see, our dad thinks he's a fairy expert, and he's writing a book. So last year, we spent the whole year going around the world with Dad and Mom looking for fairies. Afterward, we decided that even though Dad's not done with his masterpiece book yet, the only way to explain "The Trip" to other kids was to share some of his research (and our journals). So we put together our own book, *Fairypedia*. Now, there are a few things you should know about our book before you start reading it, just so you don't get confused or anything.

Chapters 1 & 2

are bits we swiped from Dad's work in progress. They'll give you general information about the Little People and then specifics about certain fairies. Dad did a pretty good job organizing (better than his sock drawer), and here you'll see:

Elemental Signs: every fairy is earth or water or air or fire and this little stamp tells you which one.

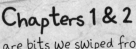

Fairy Facts: little snippets of cool information.

Fairy Fact
The word "fairy" is an English word that comes from the French *fée*, which itself came from the Latin *fatare*, "to enchant."

Enchanted Expression
"Away with the fairies"
In Gaelic folklore, travelers to the fairy realm would return believing they'd been away for mere hours—when in fact years had passed. Today, if your sister forgets your birthday, you might say she's "away with the fairies," meaning she's rather absentminded!

Enchanted Expressions: ways fairies have snuck into our language!

NEWSFLASH!
Scotland. A rade was witnessed by an 18th-century Scotsman. The fairies wore fancy clothes, rode tiny horses adorned in gold, and flashed their shiny jewels while drinking from silver goblets.

Newsflashes: stories from around the world about the fairies and the stuff they do.

Vital Stats: these boxes basically outline a fairy's personality.

VITAL STATS: Trolls
From: Germany and Scandinavia
Appearance: Larger, hairy, very ugly
Personality: Big cowardly bullies; they also have terrible table manners
Home: Alone or in small groups in remote rocky regions
Enemies: Humans, animals, and other fairies

Chapter 3

is our journals from The Trip. Some are from James and some are mine, and we also included expert background explanations from Dad's favorite guide, a yawn-inducing history of the fairies that made our eyes cross every time he read it aloud. That's why we called it Dad's Slightly Snooty and Very Boring Guidebook (or Dad's S.S.V.B.G. for short). And then there's:

Annotated Maps: show you where we went.

Wanted: cards that we wrote describing the WORST fairies from the places we visited.

Fairy Finders News: Mom collected issues from everywhere we went. It's a newspaper for people like Dad, although Dad feels "the text is too sensational to be taken seriously." James thinks he's just mad they didn't print his letter about glow-in-the-dark gnome furniture from five years ago.

Chapter 4

is full of our favorite stories, plays, and movies about fairies, written and produced by people other than our father.

So that's our book. Mom and Dad don't know, so seriously, be careful what you do with it. Otherwise we'll be grounded for the rest of our lives!

Hugs,
Jenny and James

James says "hugs" is dorky. He gives you all high fives.

A Little Background on the Little People

This is the section where Dad's collected all the fairy facts and figures. He tells about what fairies actually are, where they come from, where to find them, and a little history of his enchanted, exciting—and sometimes evil—fairy friends. He's made us read this about fifty times, but that shouldn't take away from your enjoyment. After all, you're the very first readers (of the rough draft, reminds Jenny) of the *Official Durnham Guide to Fairyland!*

WHAT EXACTLY IS A FAIRY?

This is a question much like the fairy realm itself — mysterious and interpreted differently by everyone. In some mythology, the term "fairy" described only a tiny winged sprite. But today, we have less exposure to their world (and more closed minds!), and any magical creature can be considered a fairy. So whether they have wings or tails they're all fairies in our book. Welcome to Fairyland!

Define "Real"

Are fairies real? Well, across the whole world and all through time, fairies have appeared again and again in stories and personal accounts. Is this mere coincidence or rock-solid evidence? The answer is up to you.

No Glasses Necessary...

Many young people report fairy sightings, and many adults recall the sightings of their youth, even if they see no longer. Something about childhood makes finding fairies a lot easier.

The Fairy Realm

Fairies exist between, betwixt, and not quite here. We call their world the "fairy realm," but some fairies live just on the edge, where their realm blurs with our world: in nature, the sea, and even in your attic! The fairy realm has also been called the Otherworld, Avalon, the Land of the Blessed, and *Tir-na-n-Og*.

Enchanted Expression
"Away with the fairies"

In Gaelic folklore, travelers to the fairy realm would return believing they'd been away for mere hours—when in fact years had passed. Today, if your sister forgets your birthday, you might say she's "away with the fairies," meaning she's rather absentminded!

Fairy Fact

The word "fairy" is an English word that comes from the French *fée*, which itself came from the Latin *fatare*, "to enchant."

Group Dynamics

There are two types of fairies—those who live in groups, and those who prefer solitude. Fairy "troops" have been seen in many countries, mostly during their extravagant rades. (By the way, a "rade" is a procession of fairies!)

NEWSFLASH!

Scotland. A rade was witnessed by an 18th-century Scotsman. The fairies wore fancy clothes, rode tiny horses adorned in gold, and flashed their shiny jewels while drinking from silver goblets.

FAIRY FOLKLORE

Who are the fairies and where did they come from? Again, it depends on who you ask! Some say that fairies and humans used to coexist in our world and that humans once considered fairy races their Gods. Others believe fairies are creatures of the spirit world; to others they're devils or angels, ghosts or demons, and everything in between. We'll never know for sure, so the choice is up to you!

The Norse Notion

In Norse mythology, the world was shaped from the flesh and blood of the giant Ymir. His blood became the ocean and his flesh the earth, and the maggots emerging from his corpse became two races of elves: the lovely and good light elves of the sky and the shriveled and sad dark elves who live underground.

Should've Made Up Your Mind

Catholic tradition imagines that fairies were once angels who refused to take sides in the battle between God and Lucifer. For their indecision they were banished to the dark bits of the earth: some under the ocean, who became merpeople; some to barren countryside, to become leprechauns; others underground to take up residence as goblins and trolls.

Fairy Aliases

- Irish: Wee Ones, Gentry, Them Who Prowl

- Scottish: People of Peace, Prowlies, the Still Folk

- Scandinavian (Norse): Light and Dark Elves

- English: Little People, Good Folk

- Welsh: Fair Folk, Night Walkers, Them Who Be

IRELAND

Irish You'd Marry Me!

Fand, a fairy queen, wished to marry Cuchulain, her human lover. But the Irish Sea God Manaan believed that fairies and humans—who had once lived peacefully side by side—were growing apart. So he erased their memories of each other, forever ensuring that our two worlds would be separate.

NEWSFLASH!

Ireland. After 1,000 years of rule, the Tuatha De Danann Gods were conquered by invading Milesians and forced to retreat into hollow mounds and grassy hillocks. This ancient race now lives underground as gnomes and fairies, keepers of the Otherworld. This invasion occurred on May 1st (May Day), one of the most important fairy holidays!

English Evils

King James I (1566–1625) wrote more than just an updated Bible. Perhaps because he was convinced that evil beings had once tried to murder himself and his queen at sea, his tome *Daemonologie* insisted that fairies had demon roots, and should be blamed for many earthly problems—and exorcized where possible!

Great Scot!

Some Scottish fairies share similar names with traditional Scottish families. Did these groups intermarry long ago? Fairies do love bright colors, so perhaps they helped inspire those lovely kilts!

FAIRIES: GOOD, BAD & UGLY

From the dearest of friends to the fiercest of foes, fairies have as many personalities as humans do. For every important event in our lives—from births through marriage, festivals to funerals—just about every part of the world has a fairy who can help or hinder. Here are just a few of the many examples.

Good Fairies

These are the fairies we call friends and call upon in our times of need—and just when we want a bit of fun!

Give Me One Example...

Blue Ladies are translucent, sparkling fairy maidens who plant wildflowers, save humans from avalanches, and teach the sick and wounded about medicinal herbs.

They...

- Infuse life with fun and whimsy
- Protect us against negative forces
- Offer connection to nature
- Help us realize our dreams

Other Goody Two-Shoes

- Brownies (*see pp54–55*)
- Gnomes (*see pp36–37*)
- Merpeople (some of the time!) (*see pp42–43*)

Bad Fairies

If you see one of these fairies, it tends to mean that something in your life needs to change. Perhaps someone is acting cruelly toward you— or perhaps you've not been the nicest person yourself!

They...
- Create chaos in our lives
- Disrupt our sleep and dreams
- Cause nightmares and depression
- Harm people and other fairies

Give Me One Example...

Boggarts are squat, disfigured household fairies who delight in breaking everyday items, rearranging furniture, making the phone ring at odd hours, and generally driving humans crazy.

Other Meanies
- Water Horses
  (*see pp38–39*)
- Trolls
  (*see pp52–53*)
- Ogres
  (*see pp50–51*)

Fairy Fact

"Goblin" is a generic term for a dark and mean-spirited fairy.

The Ugly?

Just like a pretty red apple that disguises a wormy center, the appearance of a fairy may mask its true intentions. The ugliest fairy could be the one who deserves a hug, while the loveliest may be truly nasty. Some fairies whose appearances may not tell the whole story include the following:

- Hobgoblins (*see pp48–49*) are ugly household dwarves that can be as nice as brownies!

- Giants (*see pp50–51*) may look terrifying, but they are often friendly, and are even afraid of cats!

- Sylvans are beautiful Greek fairies who cause accident and mortal injury to forest travelers.

CREEPY CHANGELINGS

Changelings are human babies who have been stolen by fairies and replaced with sickly fairy children. Some scientific folk imagine that, in times before modern medicine, people used the changeling idea to explain why some children failed to thrive, or behaved rudely and irrationally. Whatever the truth, stories of devious fairy babies are found throughout the fairy literature, the world over.

Give Me One Good Reason...

But why would a fairy steal a human baby? Here are four popular theories:

1. To keep their bloodlines healthy, fairies must occasionally interbreed.
2. Dark and hairy fairies are entranced by beautiful, golden-haired babies.
3. Every seven years, fairies must pay a tithe of human blood to Hell.
4. Human happiness makes fairies jealous and wrathful.

It's A Changeling If...

S/he has a voracious appetite, a fondness for dancing, unnaturally quick development, a malicious temper, overall unpleasantness, greenish skin, messy hair. And, remember, if you cut a changeling's hair one day, it will have grown back by the next!

Fairies That Steal Children

Churel—India
Bendith Y Mamau—Wales
Elk—Armenia
Gello—Greece
Frau Holle—Germany
Huldre—Scandinavia
Korrigans—Brittany (Northern France)
Lake Demons—Spain
Sukusendal—Finland
Sidhe—Ireland
Ogbanje—Nigeria
Anhanga—Brazil
Abiku—Yoruba people of West Africa
Apc'Inic—Canada
Bogie—Britain

Changeling Case Files: Baby Of Breslau

In 1580, a farm woman had just given birth, and brought her baby to the fields while she helped make hay for the village nobleman. When she returned to nurse it, the baby suckled so greedily and made such screeching cries that she was sure it was a changeling. She kept the baby another few days, but it grew so ill-tempered that she was positive of the swap. The nobleman advised her to take the baby to the field and beat it with a switch—and eventually it wailed so loudly that the fairies arrived, took their baby back, and returned her child.

Changeling Cures

If you suspect a loved one has been changed, DO NOT beat it with a switch! There are more effective and humane treatments, which will lead to the same result: a changeling whose true nature has been revealed will disappear up the chimney, and the real baby will be found on the doorstep or sleeping in its cradle.

Realistic Remedies

- Plant garlic or herbs under the crib
- Have the baby sneeze three times in a row
- Place iron or steel under the bed
- Clip an iron pin on its clothing
- Put its clothes on inside out
- Hang a rowan branch over its cradle
- Wrap the baby in its father's shirt
- Cause the baby to laugh heartily
- Scatter salt on the doorstep and windowsill

What's In A Name?

If you've read the story of *Rumpelstiltskin*, you remember that knowing a fairy's true name gives you power over it—and the same is true if a fairy knows yours. This idea is particularly common in Celtic, Semitic, and Polynesian cultures, where unnamed children are considered at risk of fairy abduction. Often the child will not be called its true name until it's five years old, when the danger is believed to have passed.

FAIRIES: SMALL TO TALL & MORE

Some fairies are so tiny they could get lost in a thimble, while others could crush a school bus with one foot—and still some are so otherworldly they don't have physical bodies at all. Rumors abound about what a fairy's size means about its personality: a common one says that small fairies are more attractive and friendlier, while larger fairies are dishonest and often baby snatchers.

Judge for yourself from the information that follows.

SCALE

- Mountain
- Formorians
- Merpeople
- Ant
- Abatwas

Gigantic Proportions

Formorians are huge, beastly sea monsters who are mean, stupid, and represent death and disease. Some speculate that these creatures are as big as mountains. They're said to be an old Irish race, eventually forced into the sea by invaders—all that fighting might explain why they each have only one leg, one hand, and one eye. Ick.

Eensy Entity

Zulu tradition says abatwa fairies are so little that they can ride ants as humans ride horses! They are shy and quite sensitive, and can only be seen by very young children, wizards, and pregnant women.

Fairy Fact

If a pregnant woman you know sees an abatwa, you can bet she'll have a baby boy!

Shape-shifting

Most fairies have the power to change shape and size, and often change into common animals, such as cows, deer, horses, and dogs. They can also manifest in nature, as trees, water, and fire, and some can even become invisible (or stay that way!).

British Balloon

A spriggan is an English fairy who is generally small and round, but can suck in huge amounts of air and inflate itself into a giant.

NEWSFLASH!

Cornwall, England. Legend here has it that each time a fairy shape-shifts, it shrinks more and more. Be careful of stepping on teeny "insects"—you might be crushing a fairy!

Fairy Fact

Most fairies live between 400 and 1,000 years, although some are immortal.

Chi Spirit

Chi is energy in the Chinese tradition. These spirits flow through bodies and homes, and many traditions—such as yoga and feng shui—exist to help *chi* move freely.

Spiritual Bodies

Some believe fairies exist only in our minds—and in certain cases, they might be right! The world over, there are spirits who have definite personalities, but no physical presence at all.

FAIRY-FINDING TRICKS & TIPS

How—you must be wondering—can you find your own fairy friends? Some believe you should simply close your eyes and believe, while others prefer more concrete tactics. Either way, fairies have some general likes, and knowing these can help bring them to you like moths to a flame—or should we say like fairies to milk and cookies?

Fairy Rings

These are natural circles made of withered grass, bright grass, or toadstools. They're found in lawns, meadows, or other grassy areas. Though some believe these rings are produced by a fungus, many believe they're formed because fairies are dancing and making merry just inside the ring. If you can't find one growing naturally, you can always make your own (*see opposite*).

To Find A Fairy...

- Keep your house clean—fairies don't like messes!
- Put out colored stones or crystals
- Plant a garden
- Create a fairy ring (*see below*)

DIY Fairy Ring

You can create a fairy ring to help you communicate with Fairyland. Here's how:

1. Trace a circle on the ground with a circumference of around 9ft (3m).
2. Walk clockwise around the circle and put herbs and flowers on its outline.
3. Step inside and summon the fairies!
4. When you're done, scatter the herbs and flowers and blend ring back into earth.

The Way To A Fairy's Heart...

Leave a delicious offering to attract household fairies. Here are a few of their favorite foods:

- Apples and other tree fruits (*see below*)
- Barley
- Blackberries
- Butter
- Cakes
- Candies
- Cheese
- Cookies
- Honey
- Milk

NEWSFLASH!

Cornwall, England. The Cornish never cry over spilled milk. Here there's no cause for scolding—spilled milk is considered a gift to the fairies!

FAIRY FACT

Most fairies love dogs, but they're not fond of cats. It's said that we began hanging bells from kitty collars to warn friendly fairies of their approaching enemy! On the flip side, pointy-eared and tail-less Manx cats from the Isle of Man may be fairies themselves—or may have been bred by them.

Mind The Fairy Harvest

Almost every fairy has a sweet tooth, and they love apples and other fruits. You should always be sure to leave the first and last piece of fruit on your fruit trees to attract fairies—it's known as the fairy harvest!

Protective Measures

As you well know, not all fairies are friendly. Here are a few tips to avoid the meanies:

- Fairies hate iron, so carry an iron horseshoe in dangerous areas. (Irish fairy forefathers were conquered in the Bronze Age by Europeans who already had superior iron weapons—hence fairies' mistrust of metals!)

- Fairies love to tangle human hair—to avoid a head of snarls, put your shoes under your bed, toes pointing out.

- Remember how to protect yourself from human-snatchers: see pages 18–19 for the full list.

Fairy Fact

Leprechauns, the Irish fairies, have always been associated with luck. But did you know that their particular love of horses has made the horseshoe a good luck symbol?

Backyard Basics

You'll learn of faraway places where fairies dwell in the *It's Elemental!* section, but here are some closer-to-home things to look for. Head outside and take a walk—and if you see these things, fairies are sure to be close by!

Oak

- Foxglove (Beware: it's poisonous!)
- Bluebells
- Jasmine
- Primrose
- Clover
- Ferns
- Thyme
- Fountains
- Birdbaths
- Oak trees

Primrose

Don't Do The Time Warp

There are many stories of humans being romanced into Fairyland as husbands or wives, and then enslaved—or of people who share a merry dance and fairy feast, only to become trapped in their world. Time in the fairy realm is different—what seems a few minutes there can be years here. So beware when reveling with fairies, lest you need a hypnotist to bring you back (thankfully, their methods are very effective).

Freaky Fridays

You might want to conduct your sprite search on a Friday, the fairy Sabbath day and when fairy powers are at their peak. However, Fridays are also when fairies are most often up to tricks, looking to snatch human babies or kidnap young girls to be their brides. A related warning: don't get married or start new job on a Friday, for fairy mischief might interfere!

Spotting Shape-shifters

Are the animals around you fairies in disguise? Fairy women often choose to become red deer, and white cows are popular among all fairies—even your pet might be a fairy. But don't worry, you'll be sure to know if something's off about Fido, since shape-shifted fairies always have something unusual about their appearance: pointy ears, webbed feet, squinty eyes—look carefully and you'll see the clue!

NEWSFLASH!

Eastern Europe. Sometimes a real animal can help you find a fairy. Eastern Europeans say that dogs with white rings around their necks are being ridden by fairies!

Little Folk Loves

Seeing fairies might be as easy as paying attention to their beloved places and hobbies. Here are some of their favorite things:

- Music
- Nature
- Hunting
- Mischief
- Dancing
- Horses
- Teasing humans
- Jewels
- Brightly colored clothing
- The sound of roosters crowing

IT'S ELEMENTAL!

The theory that the world is composed of four elements—earth, air, water, and fire—originally came from the Greeks, but the first man to classify the creatures associated with each element was Paracelsus, a 16th-century philosopher. Thanks to Dr. P., we now have natural explanations for the dispositions of our fairy friends—which are quite closely related to their elements. Read on for more information about fairies and their elements.

EARTH FAIRY

Earth Fairies

These are the most numerous of all the elemental fairies. As the earth is solid and provides fertile soils for growth, earth fairies are known for their stability and have strong connections with plants, trees, flowers, roots, and minerals. They are the keepers of the earth's health and can help humans with the energies said to "ground" us—both mentally and physically.

Who They Are

- Brownies
- Gnomes
- Goblins
- Trolls
- Boggarts
- Elves
- Hobgoblins
- Leprechauns
- Forest fairies
- Dryads

Where They Live

- Forests and gardens
- Mountains and glens
- Meadows and fields
- Rock outcroppings
- Fruit orchards
- Berry patches and thickets
- Caves and mines
- Tree roots and burrows

No Littering!

Earth fairies are generally willing to lend humans a hand—if the humans are considerate and responsible with nature.

Air Fairies

Air is associated with creative spirit, and air fairies are known to help humans with invention, inspiration, and innovation. Like their element, air fairies flit around like breath and whispers; they're delicate and often have wings. Some cultures explain weather patterns, especially storms and hurricanes, as the work of air fairies.

Who They Are

- Sylphs
- Pixies
- Storm spirits
- Silkies
- Chi spirits
- Dybbuk
- Giants
- Ogres
- Pillywiggens (flower fairies)
- Genies (jinn)

Where They Live

- On mountain tops
- In the clouds
- In the air all around

Pretty Winged Things

The classic fairy image shows a girl with gossamer wings. This notion first became popular in Victorian times, when painters romanticized the flying air fairy. Cicely Mary Barker has painted thousands of such beautiful pillywiggens in her *Flower Fairies* collection—but we know that not all fairies, and not even all air fairies, are such lovely little ladies!

Enchanted Expression

"A dybbuk must have gotten into me"

Dybbuks are air fairies with no form—they are spirits who possess human bodies to make them perform mischievous or evil deeds.

Water Fairies

The water fairy population is second only to that of the earth fairies. Just like the element in which they live, water fairies are fluid beings (many are shape-shifters). They direct and control the flow and course of all the planet's water, and can also help humans with their emotional states, which can be just as fluid!

WATER
FAIRY

Where They Live

- Oceans
- Rivers
- Lakes
- Fountains and waterfalls
- Marshlands and wetlands
- Underneath lily pads
- Springs and creeks
- Wells
- Raindrops

Who They Are

- Undines
- Merpeople
- Sirens
- Selkies
- Banshees
- Kelpies
- Noggles
- Snow fairies

Enchanted Expression

"Screaming like a banshee"

Banshees are Irish and Scottish water fairies whose presence foretells a tragedy, usually a death. Their eyes are always red from weeping, and their shrieking song often marks the passing of an important or holy person.

From Charming To Cunning

Water fairy temperaments vary widely—the pretty undines look like small seahorses and are quite seductive. Noggles are far sneakier creatures: they appear to be tiny gray horses, and take great joy in clogging mill wheels and chasing people into the water.

Fire Fairies

Fire fairies are considered the most powerful of all the elementals—it's said that a fire cannot be lit unless a fire fairy is present. These fairies embody the dual natures of fire: both destructive and all-consuming, as well as passionate and strong. Human love, ambition, and spirituality often has two sides as well, and fire fairies can help influence our desires—for better or worse.

FIRE
FAIRY

Who They Are

- Salamanders
- Drakes
- Dragons
- Fire sprites
- Shining ones
- Farisilles (male fire fairies)
- Schallons (female fire fairies)
- Will o' the wisps

Fairy Fact

Drakes are fire fairies that are often smelled rather than seen—they give off the stench of rotten eggs and travel through the air as streaks of fire. Masters have been known to imprison their drakes in mandrake roots!

Where They Live

- Deserts
- Remote wooded areas
- Hearths and fireplaces
- Volcanoes and hot springs
  - Hot sand and rocks in the sun
    - Places with geothermal activity

What's A Salamander?

Some say that these fire fairies are reddish, hairy beasties, but others think salamanders look just like the lizardy creatures of the same name. They live in water but can withstand desert temperatures, and sometimes appear in flames during magic rituals!

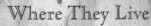

Fairy Field Guide

Now that you've read Dad's general introduction to Fairyland, James and I swiped another section for you to dig your teeth into. (James thinks that makes it sound like you're going to eat the book, but I think you know it's just an expression. Plus this book would probably taste gross.) This is Dad's favorite part, where he gets to tell you all about each of his fairies in depth: it's his mini-encyclopedia of the fairy folk. There are some nasty ones, some nice ones, and some in-betweens. I think it can be hard to know which is which, personally!

Baa Baa Beautiful

Most people say pixies are lovely, but some traditions speak of larger pixies with distorted, horsey, or goatlike features. In Ireland, these funny-looking fairies are known as "pookas."

Pixie Portrayals

- Rachael de Vienne's *Pixie Warrior*: pixies are 4-foot (1.2-m) tall females looking for human husbands, and their wings are colored by their emotions.

- J.K. Rowling's *Harry Potter and the Chamber of Secrets*: cunning Cornish blue pixies appear in Gilderoy Lockhart's Defense Against the Dark Arts class.

- Holly Black's pixies are seductive human-sized fairies with glittery wings and oodles of glam.

Pixies are pint-sized fairies

Neighborly And Never Idle

One English tale tells of a woman who disguised herself as a man and went to do her lazy husband's threshing—only to find that helpful pixies had already completed the work. Pixies hate slothful people, and have even been known to poke couch potatoes until they get up and get going!

Pixies

AIR FAIRY

The word "pixie" is sometimes used as a generic term for any fairy—incorrectly, as these little creatures are their own race. Pixie ancestors are sometimes traced to humans, so they often look like mini-people with wings—although these fairies can turn themselves into hedgehogs, which is difficult for most humans! Pixies also love to steal wild ponies, and then ride them on wild gallops while making a big, tangled mess of the animals' manes.

Pixies have large, translucent wings

Enchanted Expression
"You're pixie-led!"

These little fairies have a reputation for leading people astray—but once you realize they're turning you the wrong way, just flip your clothes inside out. This will confuse the pixies long enough for you to escape!

Praise Their Souls

Pixies were present in Great Britain since time began, but once Christianity became widely practiced, many people decided that pixies were the souls of children who had died un-baptized.

Tinkerbell

Walt Disney turned Tinkerbell into a pixie in his 1953 film *Peter Pan*. In the original play, she was simply a flying speck of light projected from offstage, but Disney's animators gave her pixie wings and a pretty, womanly figure.

VITAL STATS: Pixies

From: Great Britain

Appearance: Small with oddly large heads, translucent wings, and pointed ears/noses

Personality: Generally friendly but very capricious; love dancing and music

Home: Flower gardens, oak trees, and moors

Enemies: Iron

The Fantasy Elf

J.R.R. Tolkien's famous elves were people-sized fairies, more beautiful and wise than humans. His concept caught on, and the elves popularized in role-playing games like *Dungeons & Dragons* followed suit. These elves have long, pointy ears, and they are commonly called "fantasy elves" in order to distinguish them from the small, sprightly Shakespearean folk.

Elves often live in "troops"

Wishes Can Come True

Legend has it that buckthorn trees are popular elf hangouts. Try picking some bucky berries, sprinkling them in the shape of a circle, and then dancing inside it under the light of a full moon. Watch carefully for your elf to appear, and when he does say, "Halt and grant my boon!"—then make your wish fast, before he escapes.

Elves

In Norse mythology, there are light and dark elves (who live above and below ground, respectively); in Siberia elves haunt forests and streams; in Denmark female elves have beautiful front sides but hollow backs—and they play seductive string music to attract human men. In England, any trooping fairy can be called an elf, and in Scandinavia elves are white-clad and kind (unless you offend them!). Modern North American elves are happy little fairies who are excellent cobblers and make delicious cookies. Basically, what and who an elf is depends on where you are in the world!

EARTH FAIRY

Don't Cross An Elf!

Scandinavians looking to protect themselves against elfin meanies carve "elf crosses" (*Alfkors*, *Älvkors*, or *Ellakors*) into doors, walls, or other objects. The elf cross comes in one of two shapes: a pentagram or a basic cross. And it's often worn around the neck as a talisman, or carved into a silver plate.

Blame The Bard

Most mythological elves were human-size. Then William Shakespeare decided the fairies and elves in his plays would be teeny-tiny, and changed our idea of elf size forever. After this shrinking, illustrators began to portray elves as tiny men and women with pointed ears and stocking caps.

VITAL STATS: Elves

From: Across the world

Appearance: Depends on the origin, but most are small and chubby

Personality: Mostly kind to humans; playful, curious, and enjoy dancing in the moonlight

Home: Fields, human houses, woodlands, natural settings

Enemies: Cats; Sauron

Gnome Clothes

Gnomes are often depicted in blue or green clothing and conical red caps, said to protect their tender heads from dangerous falling acorns and twigs. Their caps are made of felt and are so cherished that their owners only remove them when bathing. Nonetheless, a trapped gnome will swap his sacred cap in return for freedom—but he'll be very angry about it!

Gnomes wear conical red caps

Garden-variety Gnomes

When a German created the first garden gnome in the mid-1800s, he couldn't have known that thousands of gardeners would become obsessed with his cheerful ceramics. Today, garden gnomes adorn yards the world over, inspiring flowers and plants to grow.

Gnome Home

Gnome parents always plant a "birthday tree" when a child is born, and the young gnome will mark a rune on the tree for each year of his life. The tree lives until the gnome dies, which makes it a great home for him—but useless to lumberjacks, since even a chopped-down birthday tree will live until its "gnomesake" passes on.

Gnomes

Gnomes have long been part of our popular imagination. Perhaps you remember *The World of David the Gnome*? This animated series was quite accurate as to gnome customs and habits, and was based on one of the most popular books ever written about them: *The Secret of the Gnomes*, by the Dutchman Wil Huygen. Many fairy lineages can be traced back to this race, but the most common gnomes are the kind-hearted creatures who have inspired literature, television, and even gardening!

EARTH FAIRY

Doctor Dolittles

The gnomes' main duty is to protect the forest animals that live around them, with whom they maintain close and loving relationships. So if your pet ever falls ill, turn to a gnome for help: their healing spells and knowledge of medicinal herbs are excellent.

Gnomenclature

Every country seems to have its own name for the gnome. "Gnome" itself likely came from Greek *ge-nomos*, which means "earth-dweller"—the Russian name, *Domovoi Djendoes*, also translates to "earth fairy." But the most fun term comes from the cold, snowy mountains of France and Switzerland. Here they're called *Barbegazi*, from the French *barbe-glacé*, or "frozen beard." Brr!

VITAL STATS: Gnomes

From: Europe

Appearance: Quite old; they mature by 100 years old and live to be 1,000. Most are about 6-inches (15-cm) tall and weigh around 10 ounces (285g)

Personality: Kind, jolly, clever

Home: Root systems of ancient trees (mostly oak; sometimes beech or birch)

Enemies: Martens, some owls—and lumberjacks!

Water Horses

Classic British water horses come in two flavors: the kelpies who inhabit streams and rivers, and the Each Uisge of the Scottish Highlands who live in lochs and in the sea. Make a point to avoid either type, as these beasties are cruel cannibals—they eat the fairies, humans, and deer unfortunate enough to wander close to their watery homes and fall for their conniving tricks.

WATER FAIRY

How To Spot Them

Water horses are generally black—although gray and white ones have been spotted. At first, they seem to be lost ponies, but up close their powerful bodies and dripping, seaweed-like manes give away their true nature—as does their seal-smooth skin that's as cold as death.

VITAL STATS: Water Horses

From: Great Britain, especially Scotland

Appearance: Small and bulbous horselike creatures with huge teeth, pointy ears, and seaweed manes

Personality: Sly, very mean, and sometimes murderous

Home: Lochs, rivers, streams, sea

Enemies: Unknown

Don't get on a water horse's back, or it'll drag you underwater!

Kelpie Kindness?!

Rumor has it that kelpies have helped millers keep their wheels going at night, and occasionally warn fishermen and sailors of impending storms with thunderous wails and howls.

Not Nice Nessie

Many people believe that Loch Ness's famous monster is a water horse—or at least descended from these vicious fairies. It would make sense, since water horses can live underwater.

Travel Talisman

If you plan to travel to anywhere near aquatic equines, bring a cross—traditionally, a kelpie sighting is an omen of death. But if you hitch your cross to its bridle, the kelpie will be forced to serve you . . . as your slave, instead of on its plate! It's said the MacGregor Clan has a kelpie's bridle, which also tames these beasties!

Lucky 13

These 13 sacred Celtic trees are the most common dryad homes:

- Willow
- Oak
- Birch
- Rowan
- Ash
- Alder
- Hawthorn
- Holly
- Hazel
- Vine
- Ivy
- Reed
- Elder

Dear Tooth Dryad...

A Ghillie Dhu is a male Scottish tree guardian, who wears clothes sewn of leaves and moss and lives in birch trees. Ghillie Dhu are fond of children, and some say they gather children's teeth to cast protective spells.

Dryads are beautiful fairies

Is this fairy a dryad or a hamadryad?

Nipponese Nymph

Kodama are Japanese tree spirits. Cutting down their trees is very unlucky, so a *shimenawa* (prayer rope) is often tied around the trunks of known kodama.

Dryads

A true dryad is a beautiful female fairy who charms humans from her oak tree. In fact, in ancient Greek, *drys* means "oak." Today, however, many people use the word "dryad" for any tree nymph. Dryads live in or very close to their leafy homes, and their lives are intertwined with the trees' health. Thus, harming a dryad tree was often brutally punished by the Greek Gods!

AIR FAIRY

Walking Willow

Willow trees that house dryads actually walk about at night to find new locations. Hamadryads are uber-dryads: they don't just live in trees, they are trees—at least from the waist down.

Pangs Of Love

Apollo, God of War and an excellent archer, made the mistake of teasing Eros about his silly love arrows. So Eros made two special arrows to show off his power—one to cause repulsion and the other adoration. The first struck Daphne and the second Apollo, who pursued the uninterested girl until she begged her father Peneus, the River God, for help. He turned his daughter into laurel tree, and Apollo would forever cherish this hamadryad (*see above*).

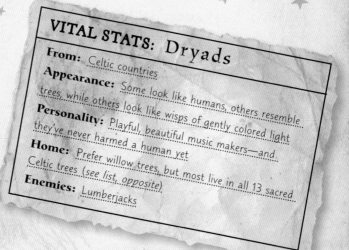

VITAL STATS: Dryads

From: Celtic countries
Appearance: Some look like humans, others resemble trees, while others look like wisps of gently colored light
Personality: Playful, beautiful music makers—and they've never harmed a human yet
Home: Prefer willow trees, but most live in all 13 sacred Celtic trees (see list, opposite)
Enemies: Lumberjacks

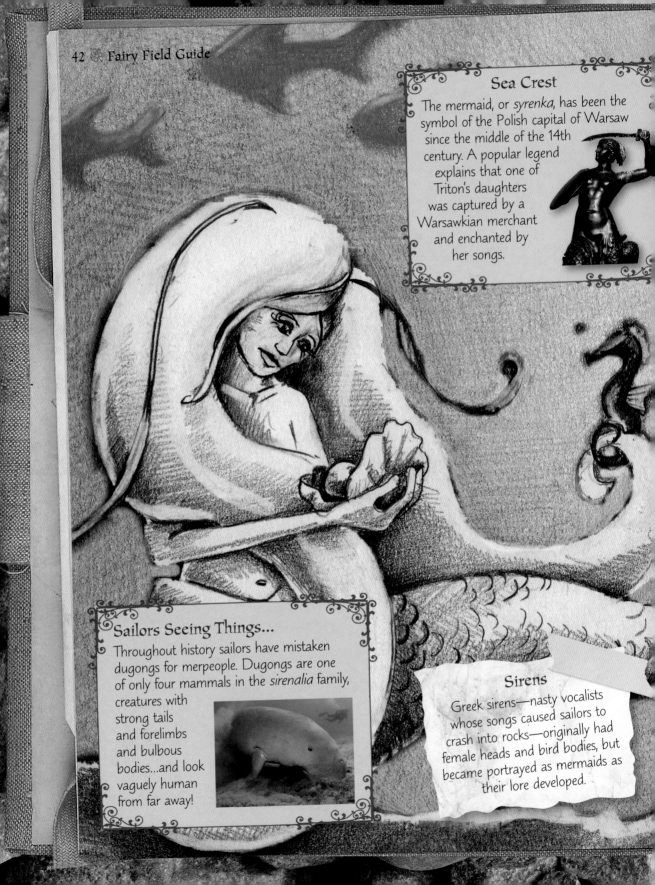

Sea Crest

The mermaid, or *syrenka*, has been the symbol of the Polish capital of Warsaw since the middle of the 14th century. A popular legend explains that one of Triton's daughters was captured by a Warsawkian merchant and enchanted by her songs.

Sailors Seeing Things...

Throughout history sailors have mistaken dugongs for merpeople. Dugongs are one of only four mammals in the *sirenalia* family, creatures with strong tails and forelimbs and bulbous bodies...and look vaguely human from far away!

Sirens

Greek sirens—nasty vocalists whose songs caused sailors to crash into rocks—originally had female heads and bird bodies, but became portrayed as mermaids as their lore developed.

Merpeople

Merpeople look human…until you spot their fishy tails! Scots say human legs exist under the scales, so that merpeople can walk on land. The term "mermaid" (for a female) might come from the French *mer*, meaning sea, or it could be a compound of *mere*, the Old English word for "sea," and "maid." No matter what the origin of our English word, tales of merpeople are nearly universal. The first known merfolk stories appeared in Assyria, around 1000 BC, and these fish people have been swimming from Cameroon to the Caribbean ever since.

Caution: Personalities May Vary

Some sailors tell of mermaids who save drowning people or steer ships clear of disaster, but others report mermaids who cause plank-walking and aquatic accidents…or, worst of all, use their bewitching voices to lure boats toward rocks and certain death.

WATER FAIRY

VITAL STATS: Merpeople

From: Across the world

Appearance: Beautiful creatures with the lower bodies of fish and upper bodies of humans

Personality: Generally vain, generally friendly—but there are exceptions to every rule

Home: Ghost ships, sunken wrecks, underwater castles

Enemies: Careless fishermen and water polluters

Leprechauns

A leprechaun is a wily little fairy who hates giving up his treasure—if you've ever discovered a pot of gold, you'll have noticed this wee guardian's temper! These little folk tend to keep to themselves, although it's said that leprechauns can be excellent conversationalists if you manage to strike up a chat. Don't bother asking for a new pair of boots, however: although they're superb shoemakers, leprechauns flat-out refuse to make more than one shoe in a "pair."

Goddess, Give Me Gold

The leprechaun's "pot of gold" derives from Crone Goddess worship. In this pagan tradition, learning to control a leprechaun meant you got the cauldron, its treasure, and three wishes—but Crone worshippers felt this payoff was more important as a spiritual achievement than a material one.

EARTH FAIRY

VITAL STATS: Leprechauns

From: Ireland, as are most treasure-hoarding fairies

Appearance: Little men in fancy green clothing, green tri-cornered hats, silver-buckled shoes

Personality: Tricky solitary fairy, always male, keeps to himself unless there's a party

Home: Large grassy hills, under roots of trees, in deserted castles, the ends of rainbows

Enemies: People who try to steal their gold; elves

Your Money's No Good Here

A leprechaun carries two leather pouches, one with a magical coin that reappears in the pouch every time he parts with it and the other containing a gold coin that turns to leaves or ashes once he gives it away. So don't accept a bribe from either purse...it won't make you any richer!

May I Have This Dance?

If you can start a leprechaun dancing, he'll have to boogie until you stop the music. Tell him you'll keep playing until he leads you to his treasure, and he'll be so annoyed by his involuntary jig that he might do just that!

Leprechauns only make one shoe in a pair!

Remember, Greed Is A Sin...

If you do find his gold and get three wishes, don't fall for the leprechaun's sneaky trick. He'll try to convince you to make a fourth wish before sundown, and if you do you'll lose everything—the spoils of all your wishes and the sparkly treasure!

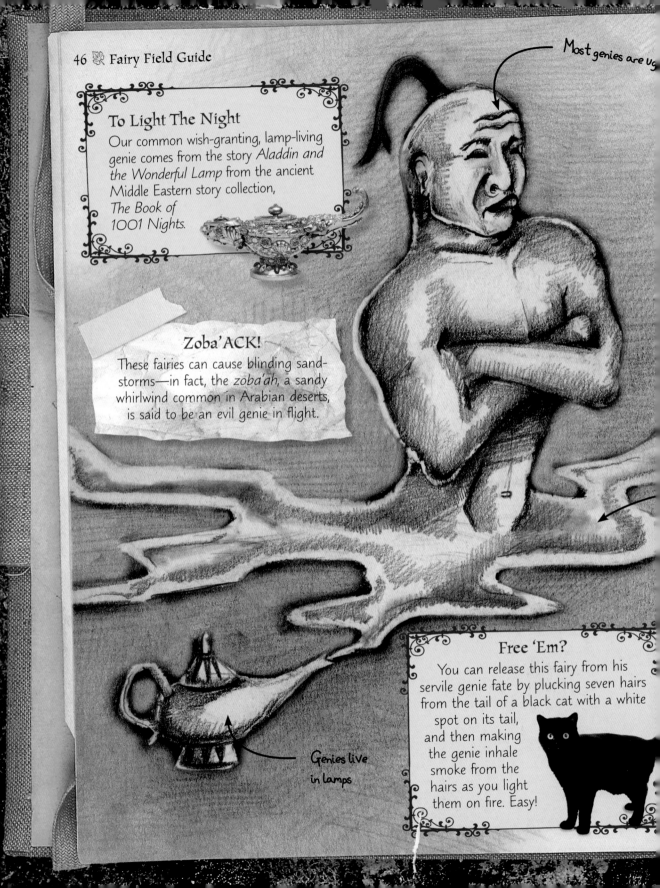

To Light The Night

Our common wish-granting, lamp-living genie comes from the story *Aladdin and the Wonderful Lamp* from the ancient Middle Eastern story collection, *The Book of 1001 Nights.*

Most genies are ug

Zoba'ACK!

These fairies can cause blinding sand-storms—in fact, the *zoba'ah*, a sandy whirlwind common in Arabian deserts, is said to be an evil genie in flight.

Genies live in lamps

Free 'Em?

You can release this fairy from his servile genie fate by plucking seven hairs from the tail of a black cat with a white spot on its tail, and then making the genie inhale smoke from the hairs as you light them on fire. Easy!

Genies

Genies (jinn) are fairies that originated in Persia and filled an entire chapter of the Koran—Al-Jinn. The word jinn became the Western "genie" through a French translation of *The Book of 1001 Nights*, as *génie* was a match in both sound and meaning. These powerful, supernatural beings are said to be formed of "smokeless fire," with fire—instead of blood—flowing in their veins. And in Arab and Muslim folklore, they're mostly ugly genie meanies, but some good jinn are also mentioned.

Exotic Vacation Destinations

In Persian mythology, genies (jinn) come from Jinnistan, a land which contains the Country of Delight and the City of Jewels. Other traditions say jinn and other fairies live in a mysterious range of mountains surrounding earth, called the Kaf.

These fairies are formed of smokeless fire!

AIR FAIRY

Be Careful What You Wish For

Three wishes sound awesome, but many wish-granting stories teach a moral: greed can have terrible—sometimes fatal—consequences. Consider Mr. White in W.W. Jacob's *The Monkey's Paw*—he wishes for £200 ($400) and gets it...as the insurance money when his son is killed in a terrible accident.

VITAL STATS: Genies

From: Saudi Arabia; Persia

Appearance: Male; shape-shifters

Personality: Nice-looking genies are nice; ugly genies are meanies

Home: Bottles and oil lamps from which they appear when summoned to grant wishes; Jinnistan

Enemies: Greedy masters; iron

The Wee Little Hobgoblin

One wee little Hobgoblin
All dressed up in red,
Was spying on a farmhouse
With mischief in his head.
"this place," said the little
   Hobgoblin,
"It could be lots of fun,
Everything's so clean and tidy,
And begging to be undone."
So the wee little Hobgoblin
He went to work with glee,
He let the cattle out the gate
And set the piglets free.
He spilled some milk in
   the kitchen,
And overturned the butterchurn.
He yanked the laundry off the line
And caused the soup to burn.
He pinched the baby and scared
   the cat
And had the mostest fun.
And when his spree was over
He said, "That's a job well done!"

Boggart Bullies

Scottish boggarts are cousins to hobgoblins, but are mean and greedy—there, the terms are used interchangeably. Boggarts will "adopt" a house and wreak havoc: they enjoy feasting on wood and can be as destructive as termites, and they also love to steal children's food. Worst of all, if a family moves to a new house to escape this fairy, he'll hide in a pot or butter churn and come along!

Hobgoblins

In most folktales, hobgoblins are cute little household fairies who hang out on warm hearths. English hobgoblins, however, are troublemakers who also spend time by the fire—while plotting their latest trick. Perhaps this change in personality occurred when the Puritans adopted the term "hobgoblin" to describe satanic forces? Of course, if you get on his bad side, even a nice hobgoblin will turn on you, so always be on your best behavior!

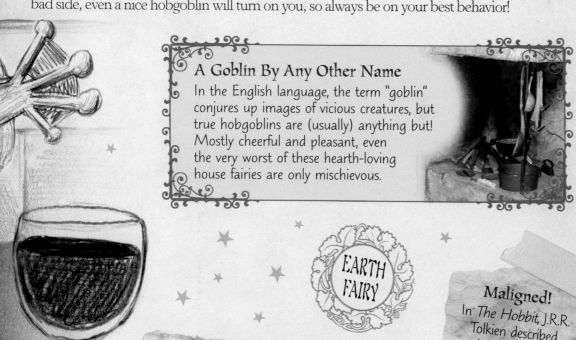

A Goblin By Any Other Name

In the English language, the term "goblin" conjures up images of vicious creatures, but true hobgoblins are (usually) anything but! Mostly cheerful and pleasant, even the very worst of these hearth-loving house fairies are only mischievous.

EARTH FAIRY

VITAL STATS: Hobgoblins

From: England, Germany, Scottish Lowlands

Appearance: Varies greatly; some are only dark blobs, others mean-looking elves

Personality: Good-natured (unless they're English); love the warmth of the fireplace

Home: Farms, especially dairies

Enemies: Unknown

Maligned!

In *The Hobbit*, J.R.R. Tolkien described hobgoblins as bigger, stronger, and scarier than goblins. After writing the book, Tolkien—who always strove to be accurate—discovered that he had reversed the truth, but some other writers still copy his mistake!

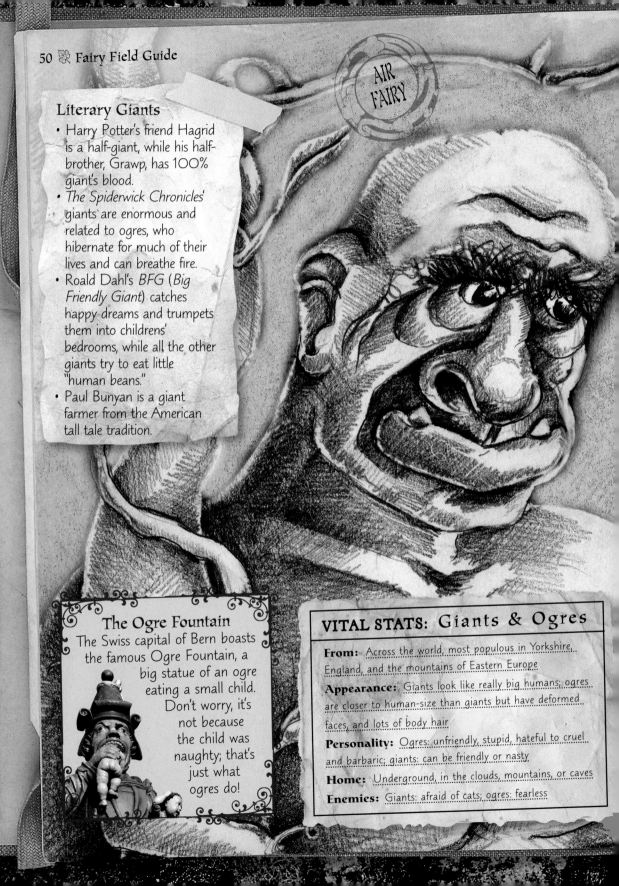

AIR FAIRY

Literary Giants

- Harry Potter's friend Hagrid is a half-giant, while his half-brother, Grawp, has 100% giant's blood.
- *The Spiderwick Chronicles'* giants are enormous and related to ogres, who hibernate for much of their lives and can breathe fire.
- Roald Dahl's *BFG* (*Big Friendly Giant*) catches happy dreams and trumpets them into childrens' bedrooms, while all the other giants try to eat little "human beans."
- Paul Bunyan is a giant farmer from the American tall tale tradition.

The Ogre Fountain

The Swiss capital of Bern boasts the famous Ogre Fountain, a big statue of an ogre eating a small child. Don't worry, it's not because the child was naughty; that's just what ogres do!

VITAL STATS: Giants & Ogres

From: Across the world, most populous in Yorkshire, England, and the mountains of Eastern Europe

Appearance: Giants look like really big humans; ogres are closer to human-size than giants but have deformed faces, and lots of body hair

Personality: Ogres: unfriendly, stupid, hateful to cruel and barbaric; giants: can be friendly or nasty

Home: Underground, in the clouds, mountains, or caves

Enemies: Giants: afraid of cats; ogres: fearless

Giants & Ogres

Every culture—from Scandinavia's Ymir to the Yak found in Thailand—seems to have tales of really big humans, some of whom are friendly and others who will not hesitate to eat you. Generally, ogres are the latter kind and giants the former, but recently, thanks to fairy tales like *Jack and the Beanstalk*, giants have been portrayed as bumbling and stupid. Our English word "giant" comes from the Greek *Gigantes*, a tribe of warmongerers who had burly-man upper bodies and legs made of serpents.

Beware The Baba

Baba Yaga is an evil and ugly Russian ogre who disguises herself as an old woman to trick small children. She enjoys suppers of yummy people (especially kids)—or, if she's too full, she'll just turn them to stone!

AIR FAIRY

Dead Now: Real Live Giants!

- A 9-foot 8-inch (2.95-m) skeleton was found near Brewersville, Indiana in 1879.
- Skeletons with jaws and teeth "twice as large as those of present day people" were discovered outside Toledo, Ohio in 1895.
- Explorer Ferdinand Magellan and his crew spotted giants in South America's Patagonia area in the late 1500s.

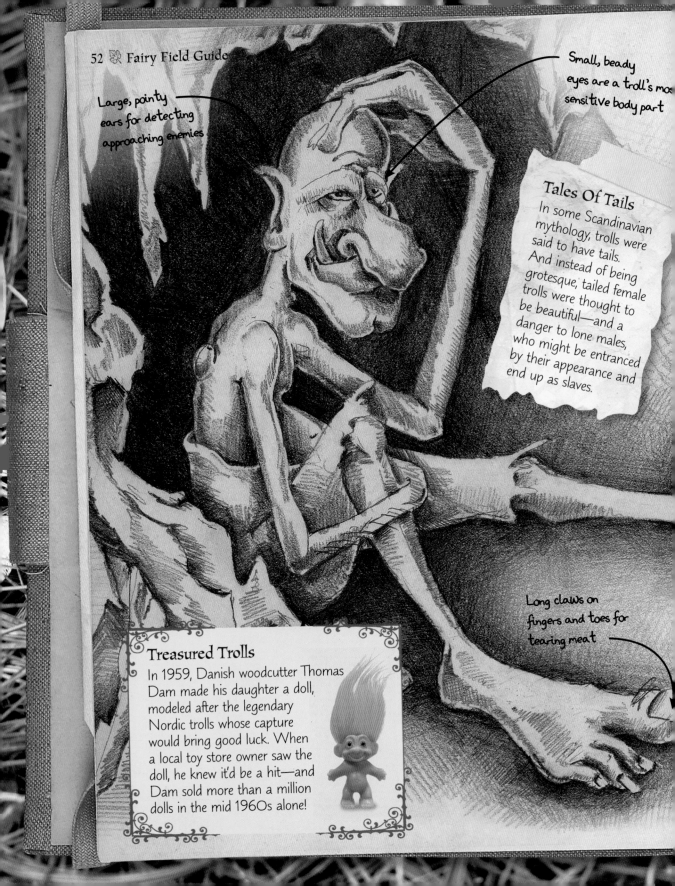

Large, pointy ears for detecting approaching enemies

Small, beady eyes are a troll's most sensitive body part

Tales Of Tails

In some Scandinavian mythology, trolls were said to have tails. And instead of being grotesque, tailed female trolls were thought to be beautiful—and a danger to lone males, who might be entranced by their appearance and end up as slaves.

Long claws on fingers and toes for tearing meat

Treasured Trolls

In 1959, Danish woodcutter Thomas Dam made his daughter a doll, modeled after the legendary Nordic trolls whose capture would bring good luck. When a local toy store owner saw the doll, he knew it'd be a hit—and Dam sold more than a million dolls in the mid 1960s alone!

Trolls

Troll lore speaks of two types—large brutish trolls with hideous tusks and cyclopic eyes from the Norse tradition, and the more human-looking underground residents common in Scandinavia. Generally, trolls are unpleasant fairies who prefer to run in packs but have no loyalty to their "tribe"—they often pick fights (oddly enough, as trolls tend to be rather cowardly). Danish Bjergfolk trolls are known to be more friendly, but even they are guilty of stealing the occasional cake or child. And if you ever take troll friends nighttime partying, remember that sunlight turns them to stone—so get them home before dawn!

Bridges And Byways

Trolls reputedly enjoy hanging out under bridges and around important byways—the better to demand money from passersby for crossing. The troll-bridge connection is so strong that even modern artists have portrayed it, as evidenced by the Bridge Troll sculpture in Seattle, Washington.

EARTH FAIRY

VITAL STATS: Trolls

From: Germany and Scandinavia

Appearance: Larger, hairy, very ugly

Personality: Big cowardly bullies; they also have terrible table manners

Home: Alone or in small groups in remote rocky regions

Enemies: Humans, animals, and other fairies

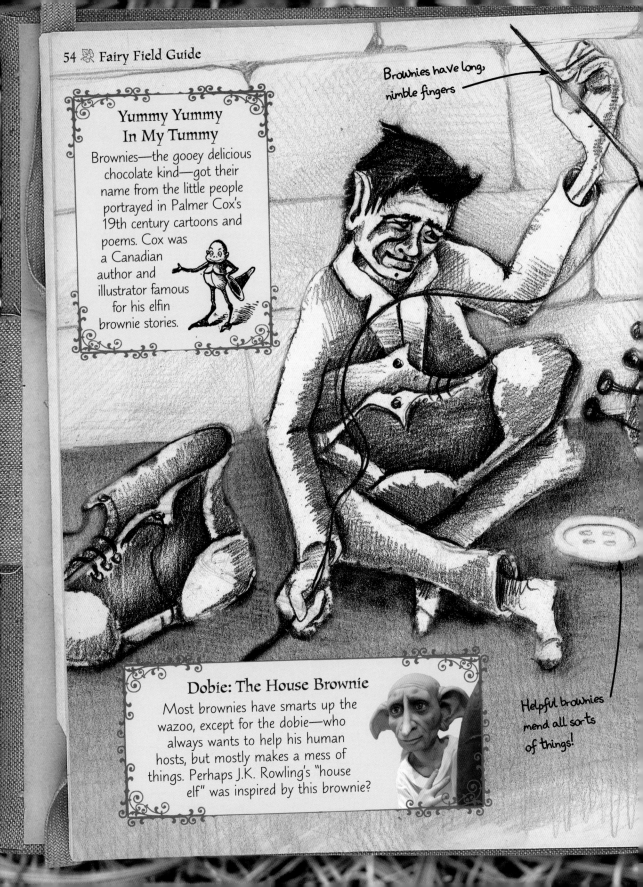

Yummy Yummy In My Tummy

Brownies—the gooey delicious chocolate kind—got their name from the little people portrayed in Palmer Cox's 19th century cartoons and poems. Cox was a Canadian author and illustrator famous for his elfin brownie stories.

Brownies have long, nimble fingers

Helpful brownies mend all sorts of things!

Dobie: The House Brownie

Most brownies have smarts up the wazoo, except for the dobie—who always wants to help his human hosts, but mostly makes a mess of things. Perhaps J.K. Rowling's "house elf" was inspired by this brownie?

Brownies

Brownies may be the nicest fairies in the realm—they'll even do your chores while you're sleeping. These fairies are completely nocturnal, and humans rarely spot them, as they prefer to stay hidden. Brownies are quite industrious, so they despise cheats, liars, and couch potatoes. And unlike their leprechaun cousins, they are excellent cobblers who make both shoes in the pair. So if you're lucky enough to have a brownie living at your house, you should celebrate!

Brownie Girl Scouts

Lord Baden-Powell, the founder of the Girl Scouts called the youngest Girl Scouts "The Brownies" after Juliana Horatia Ewing's 1870 tale. Baden-Powell wanted his scouts to be helpful as helpful can be, just like the tale's Tommy and Betty—who learn they can be industrious brownies or idle boggarts.

Brownie Etiquette

Should you want your brownie to go away, just offer him a reward for his kindness—clothes are especially irksome. He'll put them on, vanish, and never come back. But if you appreciate the little man's help, just return his goodwill and leave out some food—honey, bread, ale, and milk are his favorites.

EARTH FAIRY

Good-Night-A-Doodle-Doo

If you thought the rooster's dawn call was meant to wake humans up, you're mistaken—he crows to remind brownies that it's time for bed.

VITAL STATS: Brownies

From: Scotland, brought to North America by immigrants

Appearance: Small male dwarves, with coal black eyes, earth-colored suits of green, blue, brown, pointed ears, and long, nimble fingers

Personality: Kind, benevolent, and industrious

Home: Warm houses, attics, woodsheds, and cellars

Enemies: Cats, dogs

Fairy-finding Expedition

These are mine and Jenny's journals from the "Great Fairy Find." You might notice that I was really NOT into it at first, but if you spend enough time trying to see this stuff it's kind of amazing what you'll find. This journey convinced us that every other kid in the world should know what our dad was finding out. It was like one of those inspirational vacations you hear ladies with big hair talk about on those bad shows that come on when cartoons are over. Anyway, we hope you have as much fun reading about The Trip as we did being there!

ICELAND

Skogrsa lurking
in Sweden!

Moss People
spotted in
Germany!

NORWAY

SWEDEN

Pixies and spriggans
found in England!

Scotland

DENMARK

UNITED
KINGDOM

England

Ireland

Wales

PO

GERMANY

CZECH
REPUBLIC

ATLANTIC
OCEAN

FRANCE

AUSTRIA

ITALY

N

W   E

S

FINLAND

ROMANIA

EUROPE

This continent is basically where fairies got famous. Everywhere in the whole world has fairies, but their stories are most common here in Europe. The ancient Celts and Norse and other tribes of people who lived in what's now England and Ireland and Scotland and Iceland have passed down tons of knowledge through the ages, in spoken word and then in print and now in our dad's brain. Here comes Europe: from Dad's brain, to the airport, to some eensy hotel waaaayyyy outside of London, into our journals, and straight to you.

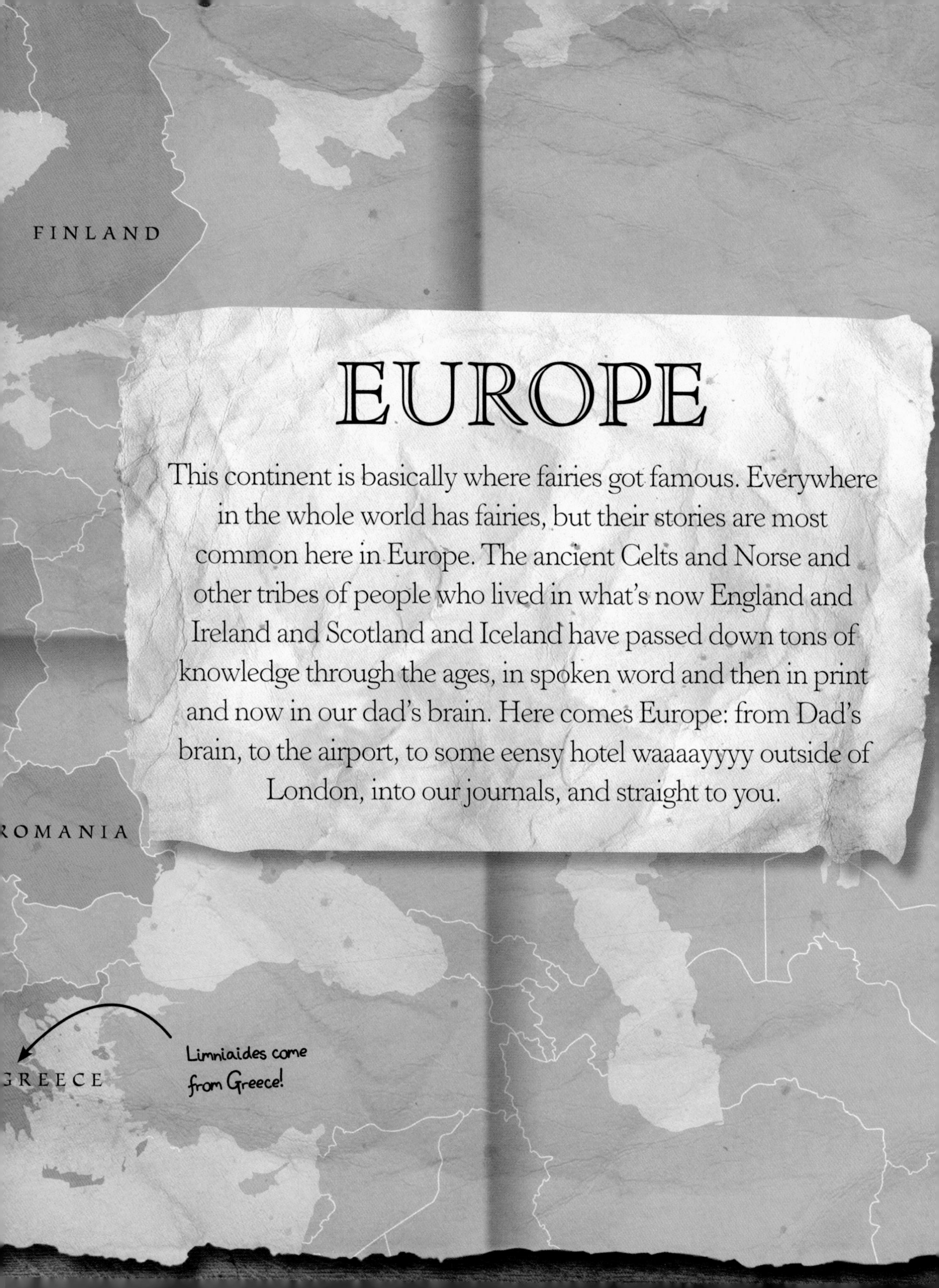

GREECE

Limniaides come from Greece!

ENGLAND

"The British Isles are rich in fairy tradition, but England has hidden much of that lore in the rhymes of *Mother Goose* and in fairy tales. However, the fairies still run rampant, as evidenced by the legends of Cornwall and the fact that Yorkshire is home to more giants and ogres than anywhere else in the world."
—From Dad's Slightly Snooty and Very Boring Guidebook

England

Fairy Fanatic:
Cicely Mary Barker (1895–1973)

This English lady wrote and painted the super-famous books about flower fairies (my sister has them all). Cicely drew each flower from careful real-life study but she swears she never saw a fairy in her whole life.

FLOWER·FAIRIES OF·THE·SUMMER

THE FAIRY STEPS

Odd Stairs In Beetham, Cumbria

Even though he's just told us how the English say they were built for fairies, I think Dad wants to climb these teeny-tiny stairs himself.

For Real

There is a town in Devon, England, called Fairy Cross. I am not kidding.

BUCKLAND ST. MARY

WANTED!
Jenny Greenteeth

The guide said DO NOT go near the River Ribble, since Jenny Greenteeth, the terrible water fairy, drowns one victim every seven years!

Pixie War!!!

This place, Buckland St. Mary, was a real-live fairy war ground. Right here pointy-eared red fairies fought with little green pixies until the red fairies were kaput.

The Rollright Stones

In Oxfordshire we saw a big rock that is supposed to be a king who ran into a witch who turned him to stone. Dad says fairies used to dance here, too, because there are lots of big important rocks called "monoliths" that are very old and spiritual.

THE KING STONE

Bincombe Down, Dorset

This town has a weird name, and there were even weirder noises at a hill there called the "singing barrows." People say they're singing fairies, and my sister totally believes them. She's a Dorkset.

FAIRY FINDERS NEWS

ENGLISH EDITION

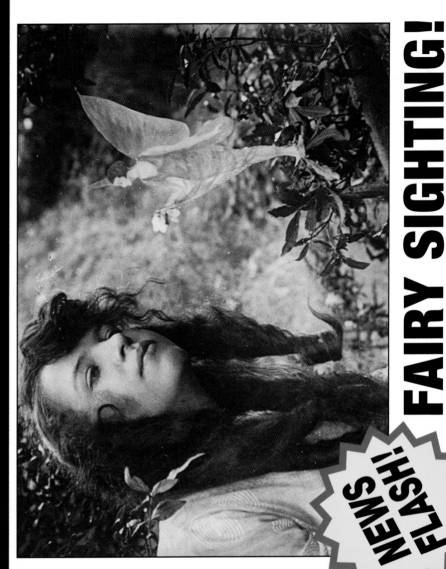

FAIRY SIGHTING!

NEWS FLASH!

A HUG TO BOTH THEIR HOUSES!

An Appeal on Behalf of Miss Griffins and Miss Wright

Dear Readers,

Of the most intriguing and wonderful photographs from Cottingley, I must beseech you to believe. You have surely read my famous and celebrated Sherlock Holmes stories—thus, you know you can trust my good judgment. I, for one, have long been certain that the Other World indeed exists—in fact, I am writing several pieces to this effect, both an article for *The Strand* entitled

WEST YORKSHIRE, ENGLAND—

Cousins Frances Griffith, 9, and Elsie Wright, 16, have captured fairies on film! The girls took two photographs of the Wee Ones in a lush village garden at Cottingley, the first of Frances with lovely frolicking sylphs and the second of Elsie with a gallant gnome. The girls reported many sightings prior to these; Frances had previously described the garden fairies as "little men dressed in green, wearing long green stocking, coats of grayish-green and matching caps."

It does not surprise this publication that skeptics are already hard at work insisting the photos were faked. This disheartening discreditation is even supported by Elsie's father, Arthur Wright, whose camera was employed to share these momentous sightings. He spoke to this reporter of the girls' active imaginations (if only he had one!) and Elsie's love of sketching fairies—certainly, he attests, the fairies are but cardboard fairy cutouts his daughter created to fool the world. What blasphemy! After speaking with the girls and seeing the photos, I must absolutely insist that he is incorrect. FFN offers its full support to Frances and Elsie in these trying times.

"Fairies Photographed" (to include the most astounding prints themselves!), and a longer work including more detail and support.

I will now make a few comments upon the two pictures, which I have studied earnestly with a high-power lens. There is an ornamental ring to the pipe of the elves which shows that the graces of art are not unknown among them. And what joy in their complete abandon of their little graceful figures as they let themselves go in the dance! They may have their shadows and trials as we have, but at least there is a great gladness manifest in the demonstration of their life.*

Yours in Belief,
Sir Arthur Conan Doyle

HISTORICAL SIGHTING OF THE MONTH

SHOCKING!!

SOMERSET, ENGLAND, 1684. FROM FFN ARCHIVES—As we well know, the world's most famous fairy market occurs in Somerset, England. This fairy phenomenon has been happening for centuries, and, luckily for FFN, one of our loyal readers spotted it! More than three hundred years ago, Richard Bovet was riding his horse by a hillside outside Blackdown when he noticed the fairies gathering at their stalls, trading, and generally making merry. He wrote they were "only slightly smaller than human beings, dressed in red, blue, and green and wearing high crowned hats."

SCOTLAND

"Scotland and Ireland share strong Celtic fairy roots. In fact, the traditional word for fairy, *sith*, is the same in both lands. Scottish fairies excel in the musical arts, and their haunting notes can be heard from the lochs to the Highlands—where many rural residents still build their cottages with the front and back doors directly opposite to allow fairy rades to easily pass through."
—From Dad's S.S.V.B.G.

Scotland

MOY CASTLE

The Two Scottish Fairy Courts

Scottish fairies have two courts, the Seelie and the Unseelie. Seelies are really nice do-gooders and they have nice parades called rades with fairy baton-twirlers. But Unseelies are from the underworld and they are MEAN and will snatch up humans and make them mean, too.

The Scariest Thing That EVER Happened To Me

My brother just told me that the wailing banshee is a fairy that warns of impending death, and then I SAW HER! This was by the river near Moy Castle, where another person saw her too way back in the 1500s—and that person died the very next day!

WANTED!
The Glaistig

She's a vampire fairy who looks beautiful until you get too close and then she's part horse and goat! She really hates boys, so I'm going to keep a close eye on my brother!

POWER PORTAL

Schiehallion

This mountain is in the center of Scotland and its name is from the Gaelic *Sidh Chailleann*, which means "Fairy Hill of the Caledonians." Our guide said it's a portal to inner earth, but the door is invisible unless you're a fairy!

Strathyre Is Fairy Country!

We stayed in Strathyre, a village surrounded by lots of hills and fairy places. My favorite place was Glen Buckie, where three fairy mounds are really close together and there are all these pebbles scattered around. They are real fairy firestones.

THE FAIRY FLAG

Flag At Dunvegan Castle

The Clan MacLeod has a ratty-tatty old flag here that they got from the fairies. If they wave it around when they're battling, they'll win, but they've done it twice before so they only have one time left.

What's A Firestone?

Firestones are rocks that can get really, really hot and stay that way. Maybe the Scottish fairies need them to warm their tiny fairy feet in the winter.

FAIRY FINDERS NEWS
SCOTTISH EDITION

EXCLUSIVE!

INSIDE: *REAL FAIRIES* PHOTOGRAPHED!

FFN OBITUARY

TRAGEDY STRIKES!

ABERFOYLE, SCOTLAND—Our Dear Reader and Beloved Friend, the Reverend Robert Kirk, is of this world no more. He was found atop Doon Hill on the 14th day of the month. Some say he simply collapsed in death, while believers know his spirit was carried off by the fairies, the "People of Peace" he so accurately portrayed in *The Secret Commonwealth of Elves, Fauns, and Fairies* (*see excerpt, below*). His 1691 work is an authority on fairy customs and habits—and a must read for all fairy-finders!

FFN editors are, however, haunted by a recent report from Rev. Kirk's cousin, Graham of Duchray. This man claims that our friend is unhappy with his fantastic fate! Duchray insists that the Reverend's said his spirit would appear at his child's baptism, where Duchray should pierce his ghostly chest with an iron dagger to release him from Fairyland. Baptism attendees indicate Kirk's ghost did arrive, but that—either from terror or surprise—Duchray failed to throw the weapon. Knowing Kirk as we did, FFN feels that the Reverend will soon realize that he is not trapped but blessed. As the seventh son of a seventh son, his connection with the fairy realm has always been great, and it is now even greater.

REVEREND ROBERT KIRK'S AMAZING FIRSTHAND ACCOUNT OF HIGHLAND FAIRIES!

Excerpt from Kirk's landmark work,
The Secret Commonwealth of Elves, Fauns, and Fairies

"[The fairies] have apparel and speech like the people of the country under which they live, so they are seen to wear plaids and various garments of the Highlands of Scotland. They speak little, and that by way of whistling, clear, not rough . . . their bodies so pliable by the subtlety of the spirits that agitate them, that they can make them appear and disappear at pleasure."

SHOCKING DETAILS

WALES

"Wales is a cradle of Celtic fairy tradition but, like England, it has lost some of its lore in modern day. Still, many Welsh speak of the fairy presence in their lives, and visitors to the land often tell of their own encounters. In fact, in 1880 Walt Sikes, US Consul to Wales, published *Welsh Fairy Lore: The Ways of the Little People Who Haunt the Vales and Woodlands.*"
—From Dad's S.S.V.B.G.

Wales

Beware The Bwairies

James and I are having a hard time pronouncing all these cool Welsh fairies' names because so many of them start with "bw." They are the Bwagonod (a shape-shifting goblin), the Bwbachs (trouble-making little house fairies), and the Bwcoid (a fast little man with glowing purple eyes). I am calling James my bwother from now on.

My Five Favorite Welsh Fairies

1. Ellyllon (elves)

2. Coblynaus (mine fairies)

3. Bwbachod (household fairies)

4. Gwragedd Annwn (water fairies)

5. Gywllion (mountain spirits)

Fairy Party Pooper

A rock door by a lake in the Brecon Beacons used to open every May Day. It led to an island invisible to mortal eyes, where fairies held parties and welcomed humans. This lasted until one human guest plucked a flower from the island. The angry fairies stole his mind, and he became a bumbling idiot for the rest of his life. Then the fairies hid the door, and it has never been opened since.

BRECON BEACONS

You've Been Warned!

A man stopped Dad on our way out of the grocery store today to warn him that fathers in families coming home from a Welsh market are sometimes found the following morning, covered in mud and mumbling to themselves, which means they were kidnapped by fairies!

Foul Folk Or Fair?

Tylwyth Teg are supposed to live in the Cwm Y Llan valley. They might not all be moondancing child-stealers, because one of Dad's books say "tylwyth teg" is just a general term for all Welsh fairies, which translates to "fair folk." I'm kinda freaked out and don't know who to believe anymore!

ENCHANTED LAND

WANTED!
Tylwyth Teg

These fairies love to kidnap blond children. "Gwlad y Tylwyth Teg" is the land where they take them, but Welsh people also use it as a synonym for where you go when you die.

IRELAND

"More than in any other Western tradition, fairies are part of the everyday lives of Irish people. Legends, stories, sightings—and fairy species themselves—are common, cherished, and abundant. There are as many as nine different substitute terms for fairy used here (such as the Good Folk and the Wee Ones), as many Irish fear these creatures enough to refuse to speak their names aloud."

—From Dad's S.S.V.B.G.

Welcome To Ireland

When we landed at Shannon International Airport, the flight attendant said we were near little fairy hills. Dad says the airport once tried to expand the runways on top of these hills, and the workers quit to keep from making the fairies mad.

WANTED!
The Dullahan

This fairy is a headless horseman who rides a fierce black steed and carries a whip made from a spine. If he stops at your door or says your name it means you're going to die.

WICKLOW MOUNTAINS

Pooka's Hole

I slipped by this big old waterfall in the Wicklow Mountains, but I know a pooka really pushed me. Dad already told us how cruel these yellow-eyed talking horses are, and since this place is called "Pooka's Hole" it's kind of a no-brainer.

Potato Perils

After the pooka pushed me down Jenny helped me up. But then she laughed and said I should have offered the pooka a potato! Irish people say potatoes dug after sunset are the tastiest and never rot; but it's dangerous to dig for them because they're favorite pooka snacks . . .

Site Of Sheerie Sighting, County Limerick

We crossed this spooky stone bridge called Mile Bridge about ten times, because Dad wanted to see a sheerie. Sheeries are fairies who are really nasty to humans, so I think Dad's a little scared.

The Pied "Piper"

The Ganacanagh is a pipe-smoking Irish fairy. He comes out of thin air in isolated places and gets girls to fall so in love with him that they die of their love. Dad joked that he'd buy me a clay pipe like Ganacanagh's to get Mindy Smith at school to like me. I am not amused.

Clay pipes →

FAIRY FINDERS
NEWS

IRISH EDITION

TIPPERARY TREE MYSTERY!

Field Report, by Ginny VonHelderstein

There are indeed fairies in the Tipperary tree, my friends! I rented a cute little Fiat and drove toward Mahon Falls, following the excellent directions given by the Dungarvan and West Waterford Tourist Board. I can barely express the thrills running through me as I saw the tree at last, and waited my turn in line to experience the fairy prank. Of course, my Fiat rolled uphill, as did

FAIRY SIGHTING!

NEWS FLASH!

TIPPERARY, IRELAND—Never would the founders of this esteemed publication have imagined today's fairy-finding possibilities. We have just received news of The Leprechaun Watch (http://www.irelandseye.com/leprechaun/webcam.htm), a live webcam focused on the Tipperary's favorite fairy ring. The camera offers the world a chance to see the fairies frolic at this celebrated spot, "twenty-four seven" as they say nowadays. Our offices have been riveted for the past week, and one intern has been encouraged to stay at his desk until he, too, sees an Irish fairy—mostly leprechauns have been sighted, but the site reports that other Irish natives like pookas, merrows, and banshees are also possibilities. In the meantime, Intern McMann has selected the following sightings to share (many more are posted on the website):

"i saw a wee leprechaun jumping up and down on his head in the bottom left section of the grass. he was having lots of fun fun fun ! ! !"

"IT WAS FREAKY!"

TRAVELS ON IRELAND'S MAGIC ROAD

SHOCKING!!!

WATERFORD, IRELAND—Grateful thanks to the many readers who contributed to our Magic Road fund. Your contributions allowed FFN staffer Ginny VonHelderstein to visit this hallowed Irish locale. See her full report, opposite.

For new readers: The Magic Road is a stretch of highway next to Waterford's most famous fairy tree. The fairies who guard this black hawthorn get mischievous whenever a car stops there to ogle. The spot is now a favorite tourist destination.

the cars before and after me, as do all cars that stop here! The fairy energy at this incredible locale is unparalleled, and I could feel their happy laughter shivering through my veins long after the roll.

As FFN readers well know, there have been many moves by the scientific community to discredit the fairies' actions, calling their magic the result of atmospheric pressure or some electromagnetic rigmarole. Indeed, in 2004 a group of technology students brought in fancy surveying equipment and concluded that the uphill rolls are an optical illusion. Illusion, indeed! Keep the letters of support pouring in, and we will continue in our campaign to keep the belief alive. In the meantime, you will all appreciate the words local farmer Jill Donohue shared with the *Waterford News and Star*,

"... The energy from the fairy tree would interfere with those instruments—they wouldn't give an accurate reading at all!"

GERMANY & EASTERN EUROPE

"Remember, Germany was not one country until the mid-19th century, and before that was divided into more than 200 independent parts, and no written record existed until the magnificent Brothers Grimm (*see pp104–109*). Today, many fairy tale translations have been obscured by political messages, but we can still find a beautiful history deep in the words."
—From Dad's S.S.V.B.G.

GERMANY
POLAND
CZECH REPUBLIC
SLOVAKIA
AUSTRIA HUNGARY
ROMANIA

PET DRAGON

Yummy!

BLACK FOREST CAKE

My Favorite Cake Ever

It was super-chocolatey with cherries and whipped cream and it was SO delicious no human could have made it. I'm sure fairies baked it, since it was named for the nearby Black Forest, which is enchanted by fairies and by dryads who pass the night walking the trees around.

What We Learned In Germany . . .

James: Tons of German fairies have dragons as pets. How crazy is that!?
Me: German fairies are usually really hairy.

LORELEI

Musical Fairies

We are waiting by the Rhine River for the Nixen to start fiddling. They're Germanic sprites that Dad says live in a beautiful underwater kingdom. James wants to find the Lorelei, a hot-stuff fairy who sings Rhine sailors to their deaths upon the rocks.

Hey, Man!

We just got caught in a downpour, and Dad blamed it on the Hey-Hey Men. They are dwarves native to Middle and Eastern Europe who create rain and wind to annoy travelers. It worked: I'm annoyed.

HEY-HEY MAN

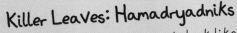

CATCHING MOSS PEOPLE

Of Milk And Moss

Dad just bought James a butterfly net, and now he is outside our chalet trying to catch German Moss People, fairies with butterfly wings. They are shy but like milk, which doesn't matter now since James just drank the glass Mom poured.

Killer Leaves: Hamadryadniks

These Slavic hamadryads look like leaves, and they really hate humans for destroying their forests. They haven't figured out how to get us yet, though, since it's hard to attack anyone when you're a leaf!

WANTED!
Gremlins

Gremlins are hairy German fairies spotted on fighter planes during World War II, where they used their tremendous strength to puncture wings and terrify pilots.

SCANDINAVIA

"Fairy mythology in Scandinavian lands descends from Norse tradition. Elves are the most populous fairies—and the Norse word for them, *alfar*, is the origin of the English 'elf.' Dwarves are also quite common in these cold lands, as are winter fairies. Even today, belief in fairy folk runs strongly through Scandinavian veins."
—From Dad's S.S.V.B.G.

ICELAND

NORWAY

FINLAND

SWEDEN

DENMARK

Why Dad Loves Iceland

He's not alone here: 10% of the Icelandic population are sure the "hidden people" exist, and another 80% refuse to rule out the possibility. I think Jenny figured out I'm now in the 80%.

Troll X-ing

We keep seeing these signs, and even my sister thinks they're cool. Even though they're mean, I kinda want to see a troll (*see pp52–53*).

A Room With A View

Tonight Dad picked a hotel room with an ocean view. According to Norse legend, if he watches the horizon at sunset, he'll see fairy islands rising for the night. The rest of us are going to bed.

SKOGRSA?

Dwarfy Business

No one knows where they meet, but of course we're looking. The Paian Dwarf Congress convene in the broader Scandinavian area to worship, play, and discuss business—like kicking out members who try to live as human beings.

Shape-shifter Scare

No one else saw the Swedish owl, but I heard him say he had something important to tell me, and now Dad is worried I've been brainwashed by a skogrsa, a shape-shifting elf who will demand my life in return for his knowledge.

WANTED!
Flygiar

These Icelandish guys pick a human, shadow you for life, and then warn you when you're about to die. If he looks calm you'll die peacefully, but if he's all bloody you will be, too. Cree-py.

Bring On The DJ!

The moon is full and we joined a whole group of fairy-seekers staring intently at piles of earth. We are in the fjords of Norway, waiting for shy little fairies called thussers to emerge and have a big fairy party. Apparently, they play excellent Norwegian folk music and love to dance!

FRANCE & ITALY

"The courtly traditions of medieval France and Italy had much influence on the fairy realm. As seen in the region's art, fairies here tend to be elegant and beautiful, no matter their size, and are more apt to make themselves known to humans than their English and Celtic counterparts. In France's Brittany, the fairy tradition is particularly strong, and many mountains, rocks, and springs are named for them."
—From Dad's S.S.V.B.G.

FRANCE

ITALY

LA DORMETTE

Get Me Out Of Mortain, France

Dad tried to convince a local to take us on a trip down a giant hole and through the underground tunnel called the "Gap of Goeblin." I wonder if goblins really live down there . . .

The Light Fantastic

Dad thinks we may have just seen some shape-shifting French fairies called lutins. Here's why: they often resemble fireflies, and we saw a whole bunch of them . . . but it's the middle of winter!

Good Night From Poitou, France

When Mom tucked me in tonight, she said the fairy La Dormette would bring me pleasant dreams, just like she does all the children in France. Dad said she would do it by throwing sand in my eyes, which I hope is not true.

FRENCH FAIRY STONE

WANTED!
Orculli

These are mean Italian giants who live on clouds and have beards and eat each other—or humans, if they have to settle for second-best.

Near Locmariaquer, France

The *Men-er-H'roeck*, or Fairy's Stone, was the largest standing monumental stone on Earth until it broke into four pieces during an 18th-century lightning storm. Dad blames the fairies for the storm, since the Bretons believe that most weird weather patterns are caused by fairies.

My Roman Souvenir

I just bought the coolest poster of a teeny fairy with backward-pointing toes riding a grasshopper. The shopkeeper said it was a Folletto, a weather-controlling fairy, and when we left the shop, it started to hail!

Folletto transport

DEAR BEFANA...

It's Like Christmas Eve, But With A New Santa Claus

But it's January 6th and James and I are watching for Befana. She's an Italian winter goddess who puts presents in good children's stockings and leaves coal for naughty ones. I wonder how she's going to fit the pony I asked for into my stocking.

GREECE

"From the beginning of Greek civilization, their tales of the Gods' wiles and whimsy have riveted audiences and terrified evildoers. Zeus and his pantheon at Mount Olympus, as well as the beasts and creatures with whom they interacted, influenced the Roman conquerors, who spread the tales across Europe and into our finest fairy traditions."
—Dad's S.S.V.B.G.

GREECE

SCYLLA AND CHARYBDIS

Hellenic Heroes

The ancient Greeks called themselves Hellens. Homer (not Bart's Dad, a Greek guy) wrote epic poems called *The Iliad* and *The Odyssey* that featured lots of otherworldly creatures.

I'm Living The Odyssey

We're following the epic sea trail of Homer's hero Odysseus, trying to find Scylla and Charybdis, the sea monsters (yes, sea monsters) near the dangerous Sirens' island home. Their music will make us drown, but Dad thinks earplugs are caution enough. Mom is nervous.

I Ate Dad's Gyro

We were eating gyros when Jenny pointed to some fireflies. Dad dropped his sandwich and ran toward the blobs of light—which were actual fireflies, and not Limniades—those Greek fairies look just the same, but they are condemned human souls.

WANTED!
Gorgons

These terrifying female monsters have fangs, and just looking at them can turn you to stone! The most famous gorgon, Medusa, had wild hair made of live serpents.

FIREFLY NOT A LIMNIADE->

CENTAUR

In The Shadows

I'm out catching snakes for Dad. Greek guardian spirits, called Stoicheion, appear as snakes and like to curl up next to warmth. So we're going to put my captives by the radiator and hope they turn back into house fairies. I can't wait!

Great Greek Fairy Beasts

- Centaurs: horse bodies, man heads
- Satyrs: goat bodies, man heads
- Cyclops: one-eyed ogre
- Sirens: sea nymphs
- Dryads: tree nymphs

THE AMERICAS

I really didn't think the Americas had any fairies until we got here. But it turns out that some of the Little People followed colonists to the New World, and then also that some peoples in the New World had their own kinds of fairies long before the colonists arrived. Up from Tierra del Fuego and through the iciest reaches of Nunavet, from the forests of California to beaches of Brazil, the Otherworld and its creatures lurk. (C'mon, Jenny, "lurk" DOES NOT make it sound too scary. Besides, those anhanga are pretty terrifying…)

CANADA

NORTH
AMERICA

UNITED STATES

Heed the geow-lud-
mo-sis-eg in Canada!

Avoid the Sasquatch
in the United States!

MEXICO

CENTRAL
AMERICA

Beware the
Brazilian anhanga!

Tepictoton on the
prowl in Mexico!

BRAZIL

PACIFIC
OCEAN

PERU

SOUTH
AMERICA

UNITED STATES & CANADA

"Northern American tradition is a fascinating blend of Native American mythology and fairy faith brought to the New World from Europe. Native totems reflect a worship of animal spirits, and many nature gods have mischievous anthropomorphic forms. Even the dragon appears on this continent—usually as a feathered snake or serpent, but with similar fire-and-wind controlling abilities."
—From Dad's S.S.V.B.G.

Fairy Stone State Park, Virginia

Legend has it that long ago, fairies danced gleefully by a spring here until an elfin messenger reported that Christ was dead. Then the fairies wept stones in the shape of crosses. Dad and I think it's cool, but James and Mom think it's a little creepy!

FAIRY STONE PARK

May-may-gway-shi love fish!

Burnt Bluff, Michigan

The Algonquian Indians painted red ocher pictographs here between 300 and 800 AD—or, legend goes, their may-may-gway-shi fairies held the brushes. These fairies love fish and water and sometimes have horns. They look a like short Bigfoots.

REAL-LIVE FAIRY FESTIVAL

Faerieworlds

This is a music fantasy arts and crafts festival. Since 2003, people searching for the "glamour of faerie" have come to Eugene, Oregon, to get glamorous together. It's past my bedtime, but I know I would love it if I could stay up.

Fairy, Texas

Dad was not happy when we got here and it turned out the town was not full of fairies. Instead, it was named after a tiny lady called Fairy Fort. She was 2 feet 7 inches (less than a meter!) and weighed about 28lbs (13kg). James suggested she might have been a dwarf—which is a fairy, Dad!

TROLL-FREE FALLS

Alberta, Canada

We just hiked through all eight of the Troll Falls. I'm tired and in a bad mood because we didn't see any trolls today.

New Brunswick, Canada

At the Tobique Reserve for the Maliseet Nation we got to talk to some Maliseet elders. They told us about geow-lud-mo-sis-eg: omen-bringing fairies. Their omens can be good or bad, depending on the reaction of the people who see them. We are leaving for South America today, so we're hoping for good omens!

WANTED! Sasquatch

Also called "Bigfoot," the Sasquatch is a giant, hairy beast who lives in the North American woods. He's 7-11 feet (2-3m) tall and, although he looks scary, he's supposed to be nice.

READERS' FAVORITE
ST. PATTY'S SIGHTING!

SPOTTED!

MOBILE, ALABAMA—On St. Patrick's Day leprechaun visitor from Ireland has been spotted in a tree in the Crichton suburb of Mobile! This FFN reporter traveled many miles to observe the incredible occasion, along with enormous crowds from surrounding areas. A local news channel released a sketch of a sprightly man in a bowler hat to help onlookers spot the Irish refugee, and a lucky sighter describes, "he was smiling, and at one point I thought he tipped his hat." This

READERS IN THE REALM!

Dear FFN,

After many years, I am finally ready to share: I have seen the fairy realm. When I was a little girl, I was picnicking in the woods, and I noticed small winged fairies glimmering and dancing. We quickly rushed away and never returned. Your magazine always makes sightings sound glamorous, but this was terrifying.

Yours,
A Grudging Believer
Mi'kmaq Reserve, Eskasoni, Nova Scotia, Canada.

leprechaun only shows himself after dark, and unsurprisingly, he flees when a flashlight is pointed his way. Clearly, our fairy friend is only trying to protect his pot of gold, which some insist must be buried under the tree. One man even carried his family's heirloom leprechaun flute to Crichton, hoping its sweet sound would lure the little man to reveal the treasure's location.

This reporter wishes we could simply admire our leprechaun's presence and join him in a delightful dancing frolic, rather than rallying behind the shameless greed of the visitor who demanded: "I wanna know where da gold at."

HISTORICAL SIGHTING OF THE MONTH

PORT ARTHUR, TEXAS, 1898. FROM FFN ARCHIVES—

Arthur Stillwell, railroad magnate and founder of Port Arthur, Texas, reports that brownies told him where to place the city. FFN note: Stillwell would go on to receive many instructions from brownies throughout his life, and would happily—and publicly—assign them credit. Some Texans were made uncomfortable by these admissions at major civic events, but we wish Arthur would have invited us.

CENTRAL & SOUTH AMERICA

"Similar to their northern counterpart, Central and South American fairies display characteristics of native and European lore. The literature of Mayan civilization speaks of dwarves and giants, and the influence of Catholicism makes Death and the Devil common fairy forms. After the Spanish Inquisition, much of that fairy tradition was lost in Europe, but it lives on in the rich mythological cultures of their once-colonies." —From Dad's S.S.V.B.G.

MEXICO

BRAZIL

PERU

DAY OF THE DEAD

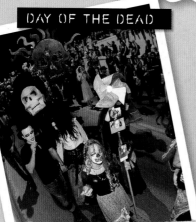

Spiders And Scorpions In A Jar, Oh My!
Well, Mom's got more to say than "Oh my!" Dad's captured some stinging insects in a jar, insisting they're tepictoton, tiny Mexican spirits who bless crops and can shape-shift into spiders and scorpions. Mom wants them OUT, now!

Mexico's Mightiest Fiesta
The Day of the Dead is a two-days-post-Halloween celebration when the living and dead have an awesome street party. Our family wasn't dancing, though; we were trying to find a jimanino. These pudgy winged fairies only appear today, and they're the souls of kids who don't know they're dead.

Uxmal, Yucatan

The Pyramid of the Magician is a temple that was built by a dwarf magician who was born from an egg. Seriously. An old witch woman found the egg, nurtured it, and then helped her teeny-tiny son build this temple overnight in order to appease the Mayan king.

ZIPS HEART DEER

My Almost Souvenir

The figures on the chessboard I wanted Mom to buy me were zips, these skinny fairies with fierce helmets and tiny spears. Their job is to protect deer—or my king, clearly!

Mexican Banshees?

Banshees don't just live in the British Isles, you know! They have them here, too—Mexicans call them cuitlapanton. These señoras have short tails, matted hair, and waddle like ducks—but they've got the same evil screams to foretell death and misfortune.

WANTED!
Anhanga

These evil Brazilian creatures are like fairy-world boogey men. They haunt travelers' dreams AND kidnap unprotected kids. Nasty!

Evil Twin Fairies!

Now Mom wants a souvenir—a fairy. Dad spent an hour convincing her not to buy bakru from a street magician: they look like babies with giant heads, are half wooden, half flesh, and only come in pairs—and are more mischievous than Jenny.

THE MIDDLE EAST & AFRICA

Dad wanted to know so much more about the fairies of all these huge places in the world, but he found the research hard-going. He doesn't speak many native African dialects (actually, he doesn't speak ANY), and most of their incredible stories still haven't been written down. If he had another life, Mom says, Dad would learn Swahili and Gbaya and Mandinka and also languages from further north, like Turkish and Arabic, and then he'd be the Brother Grimm of the modern world, gathering all the stories into a big volume for posterity (which means for everyone else for ever and ever).

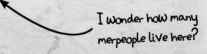

I wonder how many merpeople live here?

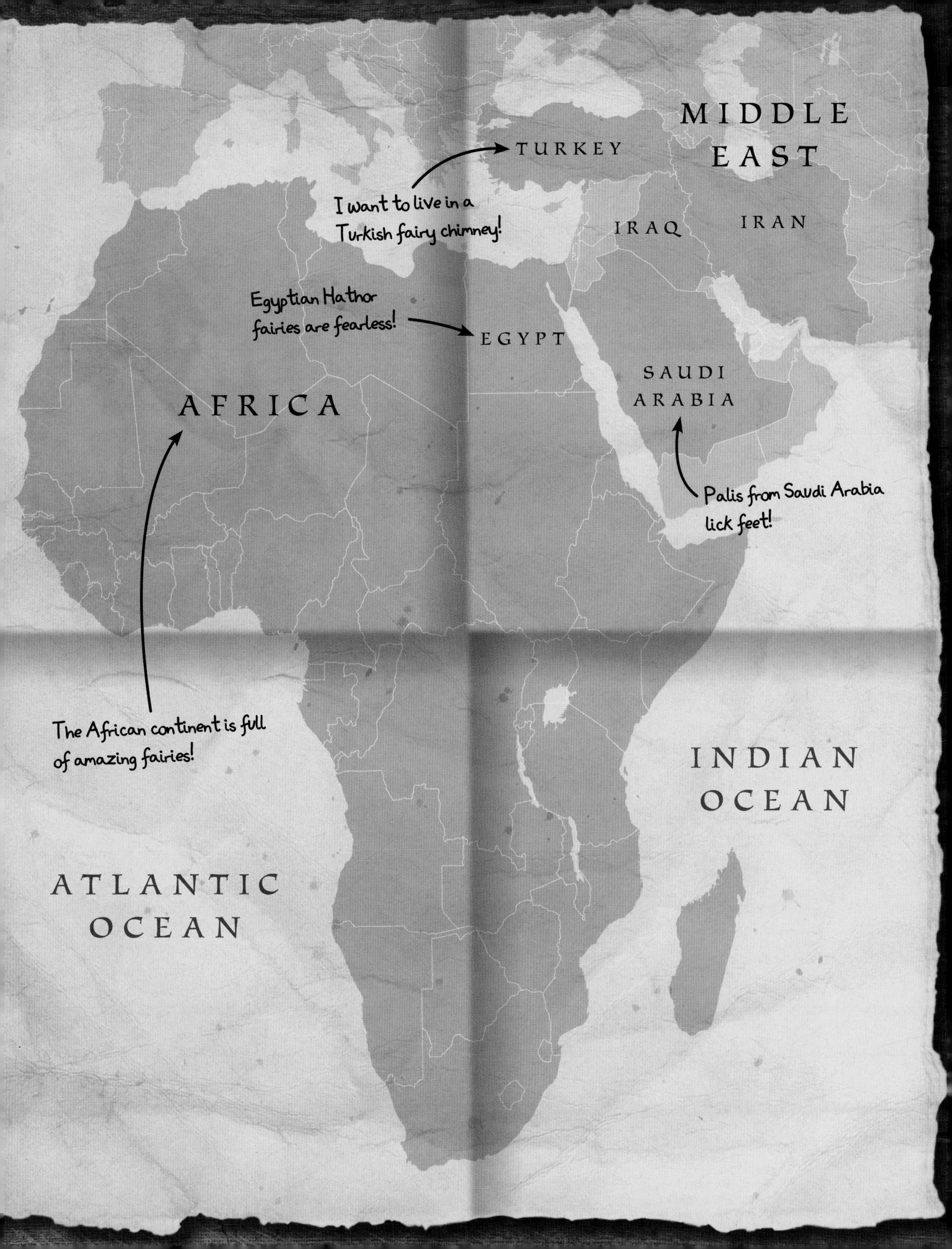

MIDDLE EAST

TURKEY

I want to live in a
Turkish fairy chimney!

IRAQ

IRAN

Egyptian Hathor
fairies are fearless!

EGYPT

SAUDI
ARABIA

AFRICA

Palis from Saudi Arabia
lick feet!

The African continent is full
of amazing fairies!

INDIAN
OCEAN

ATLANTIC
OCEAN

THE MIDDLE EAST & AFRICA

"The Middle East has a brilliant fairy history, as the desert environment bred many creatures of the Realm. Turkish fairies share much with those of the Middle East, but also include sparks of the Greek tradition. And the African continent is equally rich with Little People, especially those who explain life, death, and rebirth—their lore is also a combination of native and colonial traditions, and much has yet to be recorded."—From Dad's S.S.V.B.G.

CAPPADOCIA, TURKEY

HELLO, HATHOR

Hathor Havoc!

Because Egyptian Hathor fairies descend from Hathor, the cow-headed Goddess of the UnderWorld (and love and beauty), they aren't afraid of metals or iron. So James's pocket charm won't work against them, and he might fall in love with one!

The Fairy Chimneys

Never mind the cow-fairies, I think James should marry a Turkish girl. Then he could buy a fairy chimney house here in Turkey, where formations of hard rock sit on top of softer rock like little hats—and people live in them!

Food For Thought

I am sick of eating garlicky hummus! I'm especially jealous of the peri, the "good fairies" of Persia, who dine exclusively on perfume and other sweet-smelling things.

Dad's All-Nighter

Dad stumbled in around 5 am. He said he spent the night talking with locals, but Mom saw him reveling with the little Manzikeen fairy men, Middle-Eastern party machines who never need to sleep.

EMPTY BED!

PALIS LICK FEET

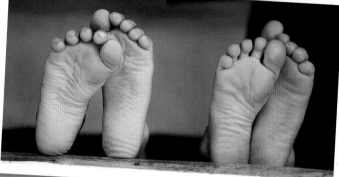

It Tickles!

We are in the Arabian desert, and the soles of my feet are pressed up against James's. This is to prevent the palis (foot-licking demon fairies) from sucking all our blood through our feet while we sleep. They are too stupid to realize what we are doing, and will think we have two heads.

James Gets A Souvenir

Mom and I are waiting for our "men" to return from a hunting expedition—they went out with the West African Dahomey tribe and their nice Aziza fairies, who give the tribe periodic practical lessons.

WANTED!
The Bori

Bori fairies are sinister West African fairy spirits. They normally appear as humans with cloven feet, but they are notorious shape-shifters!

CHINA

JAPAN

Tengu can enter your dreams in Japan!

INDIA

PACIFIC
OCEAN

THAILAND

Indian gandharvas are musical fairies!

INDIAN
OCEAN

PAPUA NEW
GUINEA

The Australian Bunyip warn of danger!

AUSTRALIA

N

W   E

S

NEW
ZEALAND

OCEANIA & ASIA

I've asked my dad six hundred times: why aren't we going searching for fairies in Antarctica? Surely he's realized it's the only continent we're missing after this bit of the journey. This seems unfair to the really cold fur-wearing fairies of Way Down Under, which I am sure exist even if Jenny can't find them on Google and my father refuses to go searching since we've been traveling for ten months already. Wait, seriously? I'd better find my cleats and get practicing, because the soccer league starts when we get back!

POLYNESIAN
ISLANDS

OCEANIA

"In Oceania, Polynesian and African beliefs fuse with Australian Aboriginal, British colonist, and New Zealand Maori tradition. Seasonal, weather, animal, and divination spirits abound, and many are said to wear native dress. How to interpret these fairies' intentions is often left up to the believer—although many of them offer much sought-after aid with hunting and rituals."
—From Dad's S.S.V.B.G.

PAPUA NEW GUINEA

POLYNESIA →

AUSTRALIA

NEW ZEALAND

My List Of Maori Fairies

The Maori people are native to New Zealand, and some fairy scholars don't realize how many fairies they have! Here are my favorites:

- Patu-paiarehe: mysterious forest-dwelling fairies
- Maero: wild, hairy, savage men-fairies of the bush
- Kahui-a-tipua: fairies with faces like dogs
- Ponaturi: sea fairies with red hair, white skin, and long, evil claws

Mad For Menihuni!

Menihuni are little fairies who wear cool tropical clothes and sometimes even help lost people. But, basically, they're Polynesian leprechauns.

WANTED!
Yama Enda

Yama Enda is a female fairy from from Papua New Guinea. She seduces men, and then turns into a tiger and devours them.

ULURU

Uluru (AKA Ayers Rock)

This huge orange-red rock is a famous hill in enormous central Australia. The Anangu Aborigines named it Uluru, and it's sacred because it rose from the bloodshed when a feast-hosting tribe felt slighted because their guests got distracted by Sleepy Lizard Women. (Yes, Dad, I meant Lizard fairies!)

I'd Definitely Let An Elf Be Their Shoemaker!

I just think it's weird: TWO fairies from this area with messed-up feet? The Australian Bunyip are nice little marsh and swamp fairies who are slimy and bark like dogs to warn humans of danger . . . but their feet are backward. And Alan are Filipino half-human, half-bird tree fairies who have fingers instead of toes (and toes instead of fingers). Yuck!

PORT FAIRY

Victoria, Australia

Now, you'd think with all his books Dad would read them. Port Fairy is a town in Victoria that got its name from the cutter *Fairy* that Captain James Wishart sailed into the port in 1827. It's a whaling station, not a wailing station.

Jenny's Future Daughter

She was going to name her Mimi until we visited Australia's Arnhem Land plateau, and discovered that Mimi are ancient Aboriginal fairy spirits who are so tall and thin that going outside on a windy day will break them in half!

ASIA

"The Asian fairy tradition has been incorporated across the world, via the ancient cultural exchange with Europe. Case in point: the Celtic word for fairy, *sith*, came from the Hindu, *siddhi*, meaning 'something which controls the elements.' And many Asian fairies do just that—from Japan's Kami nature deities, to the spirits of the region's many volcanic islands and abundant storms."
—From Dad's S.S.V.B.G.

CHINA

JAPAN

INDIA

THAILAND

OUR TRAIN

Hindu Holy Days, India

This festival is awesome! Everyone's telling us kids to find the little fairies who are supposed to be running around, so we can keep them happy by giving them sweets and tea.

INDIAN SWEETS

Musical Floors

We spent our long train ride across India with our ears on the floor—literally—trying to hear gandharvas playing their enchanting music. These musical Indian fairies are thought to live underground.

BUDDHA

Phi-Suk, Fairies Of Thailand

Mom used to be a Buddhist, so she loved these fairies, who live in nirvana with Buddha and give advice to humans on how to break out of the cycle of reincarnation.

WANTED! KAPPA

These Japanese water fairies may look funny, but look out, because they eat people! They have trunks for noses, webbed hands with claws, and turtle shells on their backs.

Chinese Fox Hunting

Dad and James are out looking for Hu Hsien, but I think it's a bit risky. Hu Hsien are mean, shape-shifting Chinese fox spirits. They often take the form of humans, and can steal the life force of unsuspecting people!

SLY FOX SPIRIT

James Found His Favorite Fairy...

It's the Japanese Tengu, a tall human-crow that has a huge, often beaklike nose, and can enter peoples' dreams. These fairies carry swords and/or feather fans to do magic, and have super-samurai skills.

TOUGH TENGU

Not So Sweet Dreams

James and I have been having bad dreams ever since we got to Japan. Dad said it's because of Baku, "The Eater of Dreams." Baku is a horrible Japanese fairy made up of a jumble of animal parts who gives people in Japan nightmares—scary!

Fairies in the Arts

We did some research for you here—James says even more than he had to do for his seventh grade report on Recurring Themes in Roman Architecture. It was weird, but searching for information you actually want to know was pretty fun. I'm not telling Mrs. Barnakles that, though. She'd assign me all sorts of extra credit work and Mom would make me do it and I'd never get to ride my pink bike with orange streamers again.

Peter Pan

In his world-famous book, *Peter Pan*, author J.M. Barrie writes whimsically of how fairies came to be: "When the first baby laughed for the first time, the laugh broke into a thousand pieces and they all went skipping about, and that was the beginning of fairies."

Tinky Beginnings

In the original play, Tinkerbell was a silent fairy who "tinkered" with pots and kettles. Tinkers are tinsmiths who mend utensils, pans, and other household items.

THE·LITTLE·WHITE·BIRD· OR ADVENTVRES·IN· KENSINGTON· GARDENS·

J·M·BARRIE·

J.M. Barrie first writes about fairies in this book

The Little White Bird

J.M. Barrie first wrote about Peter Pan in *The Little White Bird*, the tale of a bird who becomes a child, only to find himself stuck in a stroller. When he learns to fly again, he soars all the way to Neverland and meets Peter Pan. The story was also the first place Barrie wrote about fairies. He'd go on to create the fairy Tinkerbell in the play he authored to feature his now-famous Peter Pan.

J.M. Barrie was friends with Sir Arthur Conan Doyle

BARRIE

James Matthew Barrie was born in Scotland in 1860. When his older brother David died tragically at age 14, James tried to emulate David. James made such efforts to become his brother—who was their mother's favorite—that when he reached 14, he stopped growing. He married Mary Ansell in 1894. He was close friends with Sir Arthur Conan Doyle, and perhaps was inspired by that man's belief in fairies to write about them himself. Barrie died in 1937.

Selected Bibliography:

An Edinburgh Eleven **1889**
The Little White Bird **1901**
Peter Pan, or The Boy Who Wouldn't Grow Up (play) **190**
Peter and Wendy, renamed *Peter Pan* **1911**
A Kiss for Cinderella **1916**
The Boy David **1936**

Main characters	**Peter Pan**, the boy who will never grow up	**Wendy Darling**, "mother" to the Lost Boys
	Tinkerbell, the fairy whose dust helps kids fly	**Michael and John Darling**, Wendy's Brothers
	The Lost Boys, orphans who live in Neverland	**Captain Hook**, the villainous pirate

Peter Pan, the Lost Boys, and Tinkerbell all live in a place called Neverland, an island where they never have to grow up. Peter often flies to the Darling nursery to hear Mrs. Darling's tales and bring them back to the boys, who miss their own mothers' stories. On one visit, he meets Wendy, and decides she would make a great mother for the Boys. With the help of a sprinkle of Tinkerbell's fairy dust, Wendy and her brothers fly to Neverland and begin a great adventure. Tinkerbell isn't as thrilled by Wendy as the others, however—she's in love with Peter, and her jealous feelings sometimes cause the naughtier side of her fairy nature to reveal itself.

The Power Of Belief

To Barrie, people needed to believe in fairies to ensure their survival. In *Peter Pan*, Tinkerbell depends on the play's audience to revive her when she gets sick; as Peter famously pleads, "Clap your hands if you believe in fairies!"

Grimm's Fairy Tales

From trolls to fairy godmothers, and dwarves to giants, *Grimm's Fairy Tales* are rich with Little Folk. First published in 1812, these stories prove to millions of readers that people and creatures (especially fairies) aren't always what they seem to be.

Recording For Posterity

Most common fairy tales were recorded by two German brothers called Grimm. The brothers interviewed many Germans and scrutinized already published works to create a full portrait of their country's storytelling tradition. They published a grand total of 156 now very famous stories. Originally titled *Children's and Household Tales*, the book ultimately had seven editions, each of which became progressively more moralistic and less gruesome. But don't worry, you can still find the really gnarly scenes— turn the page and you'll find a couple!

Original edition of Grimm's Fairy Tales

Jack and the Beanstalk was in Grimm's

BROTHERS GRIMM

Jakob and Wilhelm Grimm were born in 1785 and 1786 in Hanau, Germany, the third and fourth sons in a family of nine. Their father was a lawyer, and both brothers studied law before they discovered their true passion: German language history and folklore tradition. During their writing careers, both brothers worked as librarians and professors. Wilhelm died in 1859, followed by Jakob in 1863. They are both buried in a cemetery in Schoenberg, and a museum in Kassel is dedicated to their scholarship and memory.

Selected Bibliography:

Children's and Household Tales 1812–1857 (7 vols)
Old German Forests 1813–1816 (3 vols)
German Legends 1816–1818 (2 vols)
Irish Fairy Tales 1826
Germany Dictionary 1856–1960 (32 vols)

Once Upon A Tree

In Grimm's *Cinderella*, there is no fairy godmother. Instead, Cinderella plants a hazel branch at her mother's grave and makes her wishes to it. Hazel trees are popular with fairies, and were even called *bile ratha* in Ireland—meaning "fairy dwelling." But where did "bibbety-bobbity-boo" come from? In fact, the *Cinderella* story recorded by Frenchman Charles Perrault in 1697—more than a century before the brothers—introduced the classic glass slippers, pumpkin carriage, and fairy godmother.

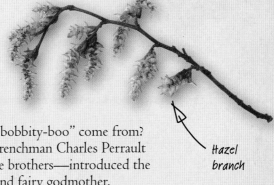

Hazel branch

World Wide Web

Many of the stories recorded by the brothers have very similar versions with roots outside of Germany. Different cultural traditions have long borrowed material from each other—and the Grimms noted that life just has some situations "so simple and natural that they reappear everywhere." For instance, the notion that a fairy godmother appears at a child's birth to bless its destiny—or curse it—is common in both France and Greece, and the basic plot of *Cinderella* is told from China to California.

Fairy godmother casting spells

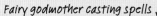

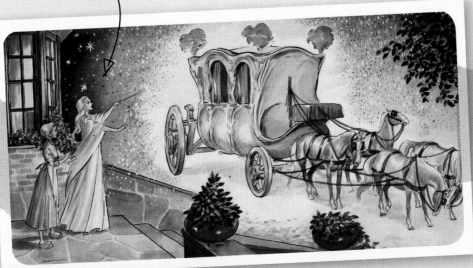

FROM *CINDERELLA*: Cinderella's new stepmother has two nasty daughters who make Cinderella's life miserable with silly chores. Luckily, our heroine has befriended the birds that flit about the hazel tree she planted on her mother's grave. These pigeons and turtledoves help Cinderella find her way to the King's ball, where the prince finds her enchanting . . .

When evening came, Cinderella wished to leave, and the King's son was anxious to go with her, but she escaped from him so quickly that he could not follow her. The King's son had, however, used a stratagem, and had caused the whole staircase to be smeared with pitch, and there, when she ran down, had the maiden's left slipper remained sticking. The King's son picked it up, and it was small and dainty, and all golden. Next morning, he went with it to the father, and said to him, "No one shall be my wife but she whose foot this golden slipper fits." Then were the two sisters glad, for they had pretty feet. The eldest went with the shoe into her room and wanted to try it on, and her mother stood by. But she could not get her big toe into it, and the shoe was too small for her. Then her mother gave her a knife and said, "Cut the toe off; when thou art Queen thou wilt have no more need to go on foot." The maiden cut the toe off, forced the foot into the shoe,

swallowed the pain, and went out to the King's son. Then he took her on his horse as his bride and rode away with her. They were, however, obliged to pass the grave, and there, on the hazel-tree, sat the two pigeons and cried,

"Turn and peep, turn and peep,
There's blood within the shoe,
The shoe it is too small for her,
The true bride waits for you."

Then he looked at her foot and saw how the blood was streaming from it. He turned his horse round and took the false bride home again, and said she was not the true one, and that the other sister was to put the shoe on. Then this one went into her chamber and got her toes safely into the shoe, but her heel was too large. So her mother gave her a knife and said, "Cut a bit off thy heel; when thou art Queen thou wilt have no more need to go on foot." The maiden cut a bit off her heel, forced her foot into the shoe, swallowed the pain, and went out to the King's son. He took her on his horse as his bride, and rode away with her, but when they passed by the hazel-tree, two little pigeons sat on it and cried,

"Turn and peep, turn and peep,
There's blood within the shoe,
The shoe it is too small for her,
The true bride waits for you."

He looked down at her foot and saw how the blood was running out of her shoe, and how it had stained her white stocking. Then he turned his horse and took the false bride home again. "This also is not the right one," said he, "have you no other daughter?" "No," said the man, "There is still a little stunted kitchen-wench which my late wife left behind her, but she cannot possibly be the bride." The King's son said he was to send her up to him; but the mother answered, "Oh, no, she is much too dirty, she cannot show herself!" He absolutely insisted on it, and Cinderella had to be called. She first washed her hands and face clean, and then went and bowed down before the King's son, who gave her the golden shoe. Then she seated herself on a stool, drew her foot out of the heavy wooden shoe, and put it into the slipper, which fitted like a glove. And when she rose up and the King's son looked at her face he recognized the beautiful maiden who had danced with him and cried, "That is the true bride!"

The step-mother and the two sisters were terrified and became pale with rage; he, however, took Cinderella on his horse and rode away with her. As they passed by the hazel-tree, the two white doves cried—

"Turn and peep, turn and peep,
No blood is in the shoe,
The shoe is not too small for her,
The true bride rides with you,"

and when they had cried that, the two came flying down and placed themselves on Cinderella's shoulders, one on the right, the other on the left, and remained sitting there. When the wedding with the King's son had to be celebrated, the two false sisters came and wanted to get into favor with Cinderella and share her good fortune. When the betrothed couple went to church, the elder was at the right side and the younger at the left, and the pigeons pecked out one eye of each of them. Afterwards as they came back, the elder was at the left, and the younger at the right, and then the pigeons pecked out the other eye of each. And thus, for their wickedness and falsehood, they were punished with blindness as long as they lived.

FROM *RUMPELSTILTSKIN*: In this story, Rumpelstiltskin is an elf who helps a poor maiden spin straw into gold. For each turn of aid, she gives the fairy a shiny gift: but when she runs out of jewelry, she promises her first born child if Rumpelstiltskin will perform his fancy trick one last time— and then the King will marry her. The elf helps, but when the child is born the Queen wants to keep it. To do so, she must guess the little man's name. Here's the rest of the story:

So the Queen thought the whole night of all the names that she had ever heard, and she sent a messenger over the country to inquire, far and wide, for any other names that there might be. When the manikin came the next day, she began with Caspar, Melchior, Balthazar, and said all the names she knew, one after another; but to every one the little man said, "That is not my name."

On the second day she had inquiries made in the neighborhood as to the names of the people there, and she repeated to the manikin the most uncommon and curious. "Perhaps your name is Shortribs, or Sheepshanks, or Laceleg?" but he always answered, "That is not my name."

On the third day the messenger came back again, and said, "I have not been able to find a single new name, but as I came to a high mountain at the end of the forest, where the fox and the hare bid each other good night, there I saw a little house, and before the house a fire was burning, and round about the fire quite a ridiculous little man was jumping: he hopped upon one leg, and shouted—

"To-day I bake, to-morrow brew,
the next I'll have the young
Queen's child.
Ha! glad am I that no one knew
that Rumpelstiltskin I am styled."

You may think how glad the Queen was when she heard the name! And when soon afterwards the little man came in, and asked, "Now, Mistress Queen, what is my name?" at first she said, "Is your name Conrad?"

"No."

"Is your name Harry?"

"No."

"Perhaps your name is Rumpelstiltskin?"

"The devil has told you that! the devil has told you that!" cried the little man, and in his anger he plunged his right foot so deep into the earth that his whole leg went in; and then in rage he pulled at his left leg so hard with both hands that he tore himself in two.

Spiderwick

The *Spiderwick Chronicles* show that the fairy realm is all around us if we only look. This five-book series recounts the amazing story of three kids who reported their experiences with all manner of Little Folk to the authors. The *Chronicles* resonate with so many believers that they have been published in 32 languages, and made into a feature film.

Spiderwick creature

One Fantastic Guide

The book that started it all is a veritable ice cream sundae of fairy lore. From teeny tiny sprites to big nasty goblins, Arthur Spiderwick tracked and recorded them all. His detailed watercolors are styled after John James Audubon's paintings—Audubon was a famous naturalist and scholar of all kinds of birds.

Spiderwick's "fantastical" guide

Tony DiTerlizzi & Holly Black

Tony DiTerlizzi was born in 1969 in South Florida and began creating fantasy art for role-playing games after he graduated from the Art Institute of Fort Lauderdale in 1992. He now lives in Massachusetts, where he creates the cool and creepy illustrations for *Spiderwick*.

Holly Black was born in 1971 and grew up in an old, creaky, and inspiring Victorian house. In 2002, her first novel *Tithe: A Modern Faerie Tale* was published. She lives in Massachusetts and has since written several more books, and not just *Spiderwick*!

DITERLIZZI & BLACK

Selected Bibliography:

The Spiderwick Chronicles
The Field Guide
The Seeing Stone
Lucinda's Secret
The Ironwood Tree
The Wrath of Mulgarath
Arthur Spiderwick's Guide to the Fantastical World Around You

After their parents separate, Jared, Simon, and Mallory Grace move to their great aunt's spooky old Victorian mansion. There they discover a hidden library—and the even more secret volume it contains, a field guide written by their distant cousin (who disappeared while trying to fool some elves). Suddenly, fairies from the guide pop up everywhere. And besides getting up to their usual mischief, certain fairies will stop at nothing to get their wee hands on the book. Why? That secret and many more are revealed in this series of the most fairy-tastic adventures imaginable: from boggarts to bridge trolls, phookas to ogres, goblins, hobgoblins, sprites, and elves, the *Spiderwick* universe contains more members of the realm than a solid-gold willow tree doused in honey!

Look through here to see fairies

The Sight

According to the Graces, fairies are only visible if you have The Sight. A few lucky bums, like the seventh son of a seventh son and people with red hair, have this ability naturally. Otherwise, some hobgoblin spit in your eye will do the trick! The Graces also suggest peeking through a rock with a hole in the middle.

Thimbletack

Thimbletack, Spiderwick mansion's household fairy, is quite the shape-shifter. He's a friendly brownie in good mood—but a boggart if he feels neglected!

The Lord of the Rings

J.R.R. Tolkien, the author of *The Lord of the Rings*, is known as the father of modern fantasy. Although it traces one epic storyline, *The Lord of the Rings* was published as a trilogy. Translated into 30 languages, it has sold millions of copies, and each book of the trilogy has been made into a feature film.

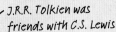

Legolas is an elf

Speaking In Elvish

Tolkien created his first language when he was thirteen—and made up several entire languages for the elves of Middle Earth, including Quenya and Sindarin. These two are studied by a group of international scholars known as the Elvish Linguistic Fellowship.

THE ROAD GOES EVER ON
a song cycle ✦ music by
donald swann ✦ poems
BY J. R. R. tolkien
SECOND EDITION REVISED

This is what Elvish looks like!

J.R.R. Tolkien was friends with C.S. Lewis

TOLKIEN

John Ronald Reuel Tolkien was born in South Africa in 1892. When their father died, his mother moved the family to her native England. During school, Tolkien's gift with languages became clear. He married Edith Bratt in 1913 and then served in the British Army during WWI, and then became a professor of English Language and Literature at Oxford University. There, he was good friends with fellow author C.S. Lewis! Tolkien had four children. His son Christopher continued to write about Middle Earth after Tolkien died in 1973.

Selected Bibliography:

The Hobbit 1938
The Lord of the Rings
  The Fellowship of the Ring 1954
  The Two Towers 1955
  The Return of the King 1956
The Silmarillion 1917–197

Main characters	Bilbo Baggins, who finds the Ring	Samwise Gamgee, Frodo's trusted friend
	Frodo Baggins, the story's hero	Aragorn, a human and heir to Gondor
	The Dark Lord Sauron, creator of the Ring	Gollum, a hobbit disfigured by the Ring
	Gandalf the Grey, a wise, powerful wizard	Saruman, a wizard corrupted by Sauron

The Dark Lord Sauron needs the One Ring of Power to conquer the world, except he lost it long ago. The One Ring has been entrusted to the hobbit Frodo Baggins by his cousin, Bilbo, who found it years before. When its importance to the fate of Middle Earth becomes clear, Frodo is forced to leave his happy home in the Shire. He must lead the eight others chosen as the Fellowship of the Ring—including a dwarf, an elf, three other hobbits, two humans, and a wizard—on a long and dangerous quest to Mount Doom, where the Dark Lord lies in wait. There Frodo must destroy the Ring in order to prevent Middle Earth from being dominated by darkness, terror, and doom . . .

Hobbits From Hobs

"Hob" is a Midland and Northern English term for fairy. Hobs are shaggy creatures who guard desolate places, and Tolkien's Hobbits were probably inspired by these fairies.

Characters from The Lord of the Rings ⟶

A Midsummer Night's Dream

One of Shakespeare's most celebrated comedies, he wrote this play between 1595 and 1596. It stars a variety of fun-loving fairies, but the most famous is the Fairy King's servant, Puck. The story's plot twists are thanks to Puck's mischief—which is meant to complicate, rather than harm.

Puck Of Many Names

Variations on this fun-loving English wood fairy called Puck were found across Europe before Shakespeare's fairy took the stage. He's known as Phooka in Ireland, Pukje in Norway, Puks in German, and Puki in Old Norse. Typically half-man and half-goat (like Greek satyrs), Puck plays sweet music on his pipes to befuddle humans. This shape-shifting fairy is also called Robin Goodfellow (the jester of the fairy court), a will o' the wisp, and even the devil.

SHAKESPEARE

William Shakespeare was born in the English town of Stratford-upon-Avon in 1564. Shakespeare married 26-year-old Anne Hathaway at the young age of 18, the two had three children, and the family moved to London while Shakespeare acted, wrote, and served as part-owner of a theater company. "The Bard," as he is sometimes known, wrote 38 plays, 154 sonnets, and a variety of poems in his lifetime. The details of Shakespeare's life are murky, but there's no doubt that his plays are some of the most famous ever written. He died in 1616.

"The Bard"

Selected Bibliography:

Romeo and Juliet 1594
Much Ado About Nothin[g] 1598
Twelfth Night 1599
Hamlet 1600
Othello 1604
Macbeth 1605

Main characters	Titania, the Fairy Queen	Hermia, who loves Lysander
	Peaseblossom, Cobweb, Moth, and Mustardseed, her fairies	Lysander, who loves Hermia
	Oberon, the Fairy King	Demetrius, who's engaged to Hermia
	Puck, Oberon's servant	Helena, who loves Demetrius

The plot of *Midsummer* is basically about love affairs and fairies, and love affairs with fairies. The thwarted lovers Hermia and Lysander decide to run off together (and are pursued by the others who love them, Helena and Demetrius), and stumble into the forest where fairy royalty are having a tiff. King Oberon wants Queen Titania's favorite servant, a changeling boy, and she won't give him over. So Oberon plays a trick on her—he tells his servant, Puck, to squeeze liquid of pansy into sleeping Titania's eyes. She'll fall in love with whomever she first sees upon waking, and while she's distracted Oberon can steal the changeling. But the Fairy King doesn't stop there—he asks Puck to meddle with the lovers, too, and soon Puck has everyone falling in love with the wrong person. Of course, they all live happily ever after—this is a romantic comedy, after all!

Word Player

English was actually simpler in Shakespeare's time than it is today: it had fewer words! To kids of that era, the Bard's words sounded normal—unless, of course, he was using a word he created, which he often did when he couldn't find one to suit his purposes. In fact, the Oxford English Dictionary credits him with more than 3,000 modern English words, such as blushing, elbow, and, eyeball!

ACT II. SCENE I. A WOOD NEAR ATHENS. Here Puck and Titania's fairy servant meet for the first time. Puck says that both Titania and Oberon are upset about the other's claim to the changeling baby, and soon the fairies' quarreling masters arrive.

Enter, from opposite sides, a FAIRY, and PUCK

PUCK
How now, spirit! whither wander you?

FAIRY
Over hill, over dale,
Thorough bush, thorough brier,
Over park, over pale,
Thorough flood, thorough fire,
I do wander everywhere,
Swifter than the moon's sphere;
And I serve the fairy queen,
To dew her orbs upon the green.
The cowslips tall her pensioners be:
In their gold coats spots you see;
Those be rubies, fairy favours,
In those freckles live their savours:
I must go seek some dewdrops here
And hang a pearl in every cowslip's ear.
Farewell, thou lob of spirits; I'll be gone:
Our queen and all our elves come
here anon.

PUCK
The king doth keep his revels here
to-night:

Take heed the queen come not within
his sight;
For Oberon is passing fell and wrath,
Because that she as her attendant hath
A lovely boy, stolen from an Indian king;
She never had so sweet a changeling;
And jealous Oberon would have
the child
Knight of his train, to trace the
forests wild;
But she perforce withholds the loved
boy,
Crowns him with flowers and makes
him all her joy:
And now they never meet in grove
or green,
By fountain clear, or spangled
starlight sheen,
But, they do square, that all their elves
for fear
Creep into acorn-cups and hide them
there.

FAIRY
Either I mistake your shape and
making quite,
Or else you are that shrewd and
knavish sprite

Call'd Robin Goodfellow: are not you he
That frights the maidens of the villagery;
Skim milk, and sometimes labour in
the quern
And bootless make the breathless house-
wife churn;
And sometime make the drink to bear
no barm;
Mislead night-wanderers, laughing at
their harm?
Those that Hobgoblin call you and
sweet Puck,
You do their work, and they shall have
good luck:
Are not you he?

PUCK
Thou speak'st aright;
I am that merry wanderer of the night.
I jest to Oberon and make him smile
When I a fat and bean-fed horse beguile,
Neighing in likeness of a filly foal:
And sometime lurk I in a gossip's bowl,
In very likeness of a roasted crab,
And when she drinks, against her
lips I bob
And on her wither'd dewlap pour the
ale.
The wisest aunt, telling the saddest tale,
Sometime for three-foot stool mistaketh
me;
Then slip I from her bum, down
topples she,
And 'tailor' cries, and falls into a cough;
And then the whole quire hold their
hips and laugh,

And waxen in their mirth and neeze and
swear
A merrier hour was never wasted there.
But, room, fairy! here comes Oberon.

FAIRY
And here my mistress. Would that he
were gone!

ACT V. SCENE I.
ATHENS. THE PALACE OF THESEUS.
[This is the final—and very famous!—
monologue from the play. Here, Puck
addresses the audience and explains that
if they've found the play upsetting,
they should imagine it was simply a
midsummer night's dream. He also
claims to be honest: what do you think?]

PUCK
If we shadows have offended,
Think but this, and all is mended,
That you have but slumber'd here
While these visions did appear.
And this weak and idle theme,
No more yielding but a dream,
Gentles, do not reprehend:
if you pardon, we will mend:
And, as I am an honest Puck,
If we have unearned luck
Now to 'scape the serpent's tongue,
We will make amends ere long;
Else the Puck a liar call;
So, good night unto you all.
Give me your hands, if we be friends,
And Robin shall restore amends.

Labyrinth

This 1986 film celebrated a place much like the fairy realm: a world "where everything seems possible and nothing is what it seems." Comic but creepy, *Labyrinth* was a collaboration between director Jim Henson, creator of the Muppets, and producer George Lucas that still has a cult following today.

That's Toby

Brian Froud

The scenes Brian Froud created as conceptual designer were inspired by his personal experiences in Fairyland. Mr. Froud has illustrated many bestselling books about fairies, all fashioned from the fairies he encounters around his home in Devon, England. And his son, Toby, played Toby in *Labyrinth*!

Jim Henson

HENSON

Jim Henson was born in 1936. He grew up in Mississippi and Maryland, and first began creating puppets during high school. He married fellow puppeteer Jane Nebel and would have five children with her. In 1963, the family moved to New York, where Jim created Muppets, Inc., and began to develop Sesame Street and his famous characters. The Muppets soon appeared on television and the big screen, where they can still be found today. He died in 1990.

Selected Films:

The Muppet Movie 1979
The Great Muppet Caper 1981
The Dark Crystal 1982
The Muppets Take Manhattan 1984

Main characters

Jareth, the Goblin King: played by David Bowie
Sarah Williams: played by Jennifer Connelly
Hoggle, a little man who helps Sarah

Ludo, a kind but bumbling beast who helps Sarah
Sir Didymus, a talking fox who helps Sarah

In a moment of aggravation, 15-year-old Sarah angrily wishes her baby brother would be kidnapped by goblins. And—oops—it works. Goblins whisk Toby away to their King's castle, at the center of a complex and befuddling labyrinth. To rescue her brother from the evil Jareth, the Goblin King, Sarah must solve the maze and reach the castle before thirteen hours have passed—or Toby will be transformed into a goblin forever. Luckily, she befriends some helpful creatures along the way!

A-Maze-ing Creatures

- Hoggle is a coward who loves plastic jewelry
- Ludo is a big, friendly, but daft beast
- Fireys are shape-shifters who swap heads with their friends
- Pixies in *Labyrinth* are nasty and bite

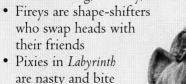

Stellar Cast

Labyrinth starred future Academy Award winner Jennifer Connolly and rock superstar David Bowie, who composed and performed the soundtrack.

To Each His Own

Every single goblin in *Labyrinth* has its own name and history, which can be found in Brian Froud's *Goblins of Labyrinth*.

The Selfish Giant

A story in Oscar Wilde's *The Happy Prince and Other Stories*, *The Selfish Giant* has been popular since its publication in 1888. It was Oscar Wilde's personal favorite, and the fairy tale he loved to read to his sons. Perhaps he wrote it to teach them about the graciousness so important in the Victorian Era (and still important today!).

Split Personalities

Wilde's son Cyril said his father would tear up when he read the tale, and when asked why, Oscar replied that really beautiful things always made him cry. Ultimately, *The Selfish Giant* shows Wilde's sweet and sentimental side, as well as a side of giants we know too well: their sometimes egotistical personalities!

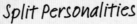

"The Selfish Giant" was published in this book

Oscar Wilde was a widely celebrated poet, playwright, and author. He was born in Dublin, Ireland in 1854. Oscar was a brilliant student and studied the Classics at Oxford University. In 1884, he married Constance Lloyd. They lived in London and had two sons, Cyril and Vyvyan. Wilde is famous for his dry humor, and always enjoyed a decadent lifestyle. In 1895, he was sentenced to two years hard labor for alleged indecency, after which he relocated to Paris. Wilde died of meningitis in 1900.

WILDE

Selected Bibliography:

The Picture of Dorian Gr
(Wilde's only novel) 189

Salomé **1893**

An Ideal Husband **1895**

The Importance of Being Earnest **1895**

The Ballad of Reading Gaol **1898**

The story begins by telling the tale of some happy children who loved to play in the Giant's garden. This was all unbeknownst to the Giant, who had been away visiting his friend, the Ogre. When he returned home, he told the children that they could not play there. He was so selfish that he put up a no-trespassing sign, and even built a wall around the garden!

After kicking the kids out out of his garden, the Giant noticed that it was always winter. One day, when the children sneaked back into the garden, the Giant heard a bird singing. He then realized that the garden needed children in order to grow into spring. He rushed outside, but they all ran in terror— except for one little boy, crying tears of distress because he couldn't climb to the top of a tree. When the Giant noticed the boy, he helped him get to the treetop, and the boy kissed him. Then the Giant flung his garden gates open wide in welcome.

The children played happily for many years, and the seasons changed, but the boy never returned. Finally, at the end of the Giant's life, the boy came back. His hands and feet were wounded, but the boy insisted they are wounds of Love, and offered to bring the Giant to his garden, Paradise. The children find the Giant later that day, dead and covered in flowers.

Index

Hi Everyone,

Dad just found this book. This is SO not good for us, so we hope you enjoyed it. It was worth it! Now we can say we wrote a book, and Jenny even thinks she saw a twinkle of pride in Mom's eye when she sent us to our rooms (with enough back issues of Fairy Finders News to last us until Dad calms down, some time next year). Keep looking for fairies—we hope you now know they're everywhere, maybe even the cupboard in your kitchen . . .or in your mom's tomato plants. But certainly outside your imagination!

From my room,
James

Resources

To learn more about fairies around the world:

A WITCH'S GUIDE TO FAERY FOLK (book)
By Edain McCoy (*Llewellyn Publications, 2002*)
THE GREAT ENCYCLOPEDIA OF FAERIES (book)
By Pierre Dubois (*Simon & Schuster, 2000*)
WORLD OF FROUD (website)
www.worldoffroud.com
THE FAIRY FAITH (film)
Written and directed by John Walker (*John Walker Productions, 2000*)

Photo Credits

DK would like to thank the following photographers for their contributions to this project. Every effort has been made to trace copyright holders. DK Publishing apologizes for any unintentional omissions, and would be pleased, if any such case should arise, to add an appropriate acknowledgment in future editions.
ABBREVIATIONS KEY: b=bottom; c=center; l=left; r=right; t=top.

AKG Images: Jonathan Barry 102 bc

Alamy: Adrian Sherratt 69bl; ALAN OLIVER 67bl; Birdlike Images Gregory Bajor 70 bl; Content Mine International 119bl; David Noton Photography 65tr, 68tr; David South 77cr; Digital Vision 79bl; Elvele Images Ltd 74bl; Glowimages RM 2-3, 126-127

Everyday Images 26br; flashover 75tl; fotoshoot 93br; Frank Chmura 44cr; imagebroker 76br; Jay Sturdevant 64bl; John Glover 22bc, 23br; Jon Arnold Images Ltd 72tl; JUPITERIMAGES/ Brand X 81cr; JUPITERIMAGES/ Polka Dot 66tl; Lebrecht Music and Arts Photo Library 16TL, 22 bl; MARKA 95br;

Mary Evans Picture Library 75tr, 80tl, 80br, 16CL, 18TL, 19TL, 25tl; Mooch Images Ltd 50bl; North Wind Picture Archives 103tr; Organics image library 22br; Paul Carstairs 21tl; Photos 12 113br; Pictorial Press Ltd 112tr, 120bc, 34bl, 19BL; Seb Rogers 69cl; Powered by Light/Alan Spencer 71tr; Rex Hughes 61tr; Robert Estall photo agency 79tr; SCPhotos 42tr; Stephen Emerson 72tr; vanneilbob 61br; wendy connett 88bl; Wildscape 60bl; A. T. Willett 88bl

AP WorldWide Images: 39cr

Bridgeman Art Library: 17BR Goblin, 1984, Ichuko, Azuma Higashi (fl.1984) / Fairy Art Museum, Tokyo, Japan; 103l Jack and the Beanstalk, Quinto, Nadir (1918-94) / Private Collection / © Look and Learn; 101tl Peter Pan and Wendy, Quinto, Nadir (1918-94) / Private Collection / © Look and Learn; 16BR The Fairy Wood (oil on canvas), Rheam, Henry Meynell (1859-1920) / Roy Miles Fine Paintings; 104br The story of Cinderella, Quinto, Nadir (1918-94) / Private Collection / © Look and Learn; 17CR The Troll, 1970, Swedish School / Private Collection ; 16BL A Gnome by Tree Roots, 1928, Rackham, Arthur (1867-1939) / Private Collection / © Chris Beetles, London, U.K.; 26 bl Brother St. Martin and the Three Trolls, 1913 (w/c on paper), Bauer, John (1882-1918) / © Nationalmuseum, Stockholm, Sweden ; 14c Etain, Helen, Maeve and Fand, Golden Deirdre's Tender Hand'' Illustration by Harry Clarke from 'Queens' by J.M. Synge pub. 1909, Clarke, Harry (1890-1931) / Private Collection / Mark Fiennes; 25b Fairies in the garden (gouache on paper), Ortiz, Jose (b.1932) / Private Collection / © Look and Learn; 114tl Robin Goodfellow, the Puck, costume design for ''A Midsummer Night's Dream'', produced by R Courtneidge at the Princes Theatre, Manchester, Wilhelm, C. (1858-1925) / Victoria & Albert Museum, London, UK; 12b The Fairy Tree (w/c), Doyle, Richard (1824-83) / Private Collection / © The Maas Gallery, London, UK; 17tl The Nightmare, 1781 (oil on canvas) (detail of 114494), Fuseli, Henry (Fussli, Johann Heinrich) (1741-1825) / The Detroit Institute of Arts, USA; 109c The Story of Rumpelstiltskin, Blasco, Jesus (1919-95) / Private Collection / © Look and Learn; 76bl The Troll and the Boy (w/c on paper), Bauer, John (1882-1918) / © Nationalmuseum, Stockholm, Sweden; 120 cl Titlepage of 'The Happy Prince and other Tales' by Oscar Wilde, 1888 (litho), Crane, Walter (1845-1915) & Hood, Jacomb (1857-1929) / Private Collection

27 cl Two fairies flying through the air, one seated on a bee and the other on a dragonfly, 1817-29 (w/c on paper), Murray, Amelia Jane (1800-1896) / Fairy Art Museum, Tokyo, Japan

Brian Froud/The Jim Henson Company: 118tl

Corbis: ALEXANDER DEMIANCHUK/Reuters/Corbis 54bc; Blue Lantern Studio 78bl; Corbis 120tr; Fine Art Photographic Library 115bl; Richard Cummins 73bl; Stapleton Collection 27tr; Stefano Bianchetti 103bc

DK Images: Barnabas Kindersley 98br; Christopher and Sally Gable 98bl; Colin Keates (c) Dorling Kindersley, Courtesy of the Natural History Museum, London 65br, 99c; Dave King (c) Dorling Kindersley, Courtesy of The Science Museum, London 21rc; David Peart 42bl; DK/Judith Miller Archive/The Estate of Cicely Mary Barker, Biblion / The Estate of Cicely Mary Barker 60cr; Geoff Dann/The British Museum/DK 14bl; James Young 41cr; Jamie Marshall 33cr, 47cr; Jane Miller 84br, 89bl; Judith Miller / Dorling Kindersley / Bucks County Antiques Center 48bc; Judith Miller / Dorling Kindersley / Gardiner Houlgate 24br; Linda Whitwam (c) CONACULTA-INAH-MEX 89tr; Philip Dowell (c) Dorling Kindersley, Courtesy of The Natural History Museum, London 50tl

Dunvegan Castle Private Collection: 65bl

From Faerieworlds: image © Pixievisions: 85tr

Getty Images: Circle of John de Critz/The Bridgeman Art Library 15bl; Peter Lilja 77tr; The Bridgeman Art Library 121c; Daryl Benson 92bl; Heinz Wohner 74br; Hulton Archive 112bc, 118 bc; Nostalgia 64br; WireImage 110bc

Jupiter Images: 10, 30, 100; Comstock 56

Library of Congress: 63bl, 101br

Courtesy of the Museum of the Gulf Coast, Port Arthur, Texas: 87bc

National Forestry Commission, UK: Shirley Leek 67br

Photo Researchers, Inc.: Keith Kent 81tr

www.naturalightphotography.ca: Rochelle Coffey 85br

Science and Society Picture Library: NmeM 62tl, 62c, 62tr

The Kobal Collection: JIM HENSON PRODUCTIONS 119tr; NICKELODEON MOVIES 110tr, 111br; RANKIN-BASS PRODUCTIONS 113br

Cover image: The Elfin Piper (pen & ink, w/c on paper), Cloke, Rene (1904-1995) / Private Collection / © Chris Beetles, London, UK / The Bridgeman Art Library

Acknowledgments

The publisher would like to thank Mark Shapiro for kind permission to print the poem *The Wee Little Hobgoblin* on page 48, and Diana Catherines for the poster design.

ALISHA NIEHAUS would like to thank Jenny, James, Frank, and Lottie Durnham for trusting her to tell their story, Shannon Beatty for her brilliant and creative editorial guidance, Bill Miller for his great design, Edain McCoy for her knowledge and enthusiasm, Chrissy McIntyre for her peerless photo finding, and Beth Sutinis for having the *Pedia* vision in the first place. Thanks also to Laura Elgin for lending her computer and zany humor to the cause, and to Danny Berger for his patience, moral support, and for always listening to the latest in gnomes with a smile.

BILL MILLER would like to thank Jessica Park and Kathy Farias for design and DTP assistance, Kellie Walsh and Rupert Rogers for the last minute notebook portrait, Caitlin Davis for sketching the creatures featured on pages 36, 45, and 48, and Danielle Delaney for the sketches on pages 32, 34, 39, 40, 42, 46, 50, 52, and 54.

SHANNON BEATTY would like to thank Edain McCoy for her expertise in advising us on all things ''fairy'', Alisha Niehaus for bringing *Fairypedia* to life, Brooke Dworkin for her eagle-eyed proofreading, Chrissy McIntyre for picture research, and Nanette Cardon the index. Thanks also to Simon Harley for his editorial assistance (and patience). To Noah and Sasha, we hope you have as much fun reading this book as we did making it.